Christian Rosencreutz, E. Foxcroft

The Hermetick Romance
The chymical wedding

ISBN/EAN: 9783337348281

Printed in Europe, USA, Canada, Australia, Japan

Cover: Foto ©Andreas Hilbeck / pixelio.de

More available books at **www.hansebooks.com**

Christian Rosencreutz, E. Foxcroft

The Hermetick Romance

The chymical wedding

THE
HERMETICK
ROMANCE:
OR THE
CHYMICAL
WEDDING:

Written in high Dutch By
Chriſtian Roſencreutz.

Tranſlated by *E. Foxcroft*, late Fellow of
Kings Colledge in *Cambridge*.

Licenſed, & Entred according to Order,

Printed, by *A. Sowle*, at the *Crooked-Billet* in Holloway-Lane *Shoreditch*: And ſold at the *Three-Kyes*
in *Nags-Head-Court Grace-Church-ſtreet*, 1690.

The Hermetick
ROMANCE, *&c.*

The First Book.

The First Day.

O N an Evening before *Easter-*
Day, I sate at a Table, and
having (as my Custom was)
in my humble Prayer sufficiently con-
versed with my Creator, and consider- Meditatio
ed many great Mysteries (whereof
the Father of Lights his Majesty had
hewn me not a few) and being now
ready to prepare in my Heart, together with my dear *Paschal Lamb*, a
small unleavened, undefiled Cake ; All
on a sudden ariseth so horrible a Tem-
pest, that I imagined no other but
that through its mighty force, the Hill
whereon my little House was founded,
would flye in pieces. But in as much
as this, and the like from the Devil
(who had done me many a spight) was
no new thing to me ; I took courage,

and

and perſiſted in my Meditation, till
ſome body (after an unuſual manner,
touched me on the Back; whereupon
I was ſo hugely terrified, that I durſt
hardly look about me; yet I ſhewed
my ſelf as cheerful as (in the like Occurrences) humane frailty would permit; Now the ſame thing ſtill twich-
ing me ſeveral times by the Coat, I
looked back, and behold it was a fair
and glorious *Lady*, whoſe Garments
were all *Skye-colour*, and curiouſly (like
Heaven) beſpangled with golden *Stars*,
in her right Hand ſhe bare a *Trumpet*
of beaten Gold, whereon a Name was
ingraven (which I could well read id)
but am as yet forbidden to reveal it.
In her left Hand ſhe had a great bundle
of *Letters* of all *Languages*, which ſhe
(as I afterwards underſtood) was to
carry into all *Countries*. She had alſo
large and beautiful *Wings*, full of *Eyes*
throughout, wherewith ſhe could mount
aloft, and flye ſwifter than any *Eagle*. I
might perhaps been able to take further notice of her, but becauſe ſhe
ſtaid ſo ſmall a time with me, and
terror and amazement ſtill poſſeſſed
me, I was fain to be content. For as

ſoon

Præconiſta.

foon as I turned about, fhe turned her *Letters* over and over, and at length drew out a fmall one, which with *great Reverence* fhe laid down upon the *Table*, and without giving one word, departed from me. But in her mounting upward, fhe gave fo mighty a *blaft* on her gallant Trumpet, that the *whole Hill* ecchoed thereof, and fer a full *quarter* of a hour after, I could hardly hear my own Words.

In fo unlooked for an adventure I was at a lofs, how either to advife, or affift my poor felf, and therefore fell upon my Knees, and *befought* my Creator to permit nothing contrary to my *Eternal* Happinefs to befall me; whereupon with fear and trembling, I went to the Letter, which was now *fo heavy*, Epiftola. as had itbeen meer Gold, it could hardly have been fo weighty. Now as I was Sigillum diligently viewing it, I found a little *Seal*, whereupon a curious Crofs with this Infcription, *IN HOC SIGNO* ✝ *VINCES*, was ingraven.

Now as foon as I efpied this Sign I was the more comforted, as not being ignorant that fuch a Seal was little acceptable, and much lefs ufeful to the

Devil.

Devil. Whereupon I tenderly opened the Letter, and within it, in an
Azure Field, in *Golden* Letters, found
the following Verfes written.

This day, this day, this, this
The Royal Wedding is.
Art thou thereto by Birth inclin'd,
And unto joy of God defign'd,
Then may'ft thou to the Mountain tend,
Whereon three ftately Temples ftand,
And there fee all from end to end.
Keep watch, and ward,
Thy felf regard ;
Unlefs with diligence thou bathe,
The Wedding can't thee harmlefs fave :
He'l dammage have that here delays ;
Let him beware, too light that weighs.

Underneath ftood *Sponfus* and *Sponfa.*

De Nuptiis. As foon as I had read this Letter, I
was prefently like to have fainted a-
way, all my Hair ftood an end, and
a cold Sweat trickled down my whole
Body. For although I well perceived
that this was the appointed *Wedding,*
whereof feven Years before I was acquainted in a *bodily Vifion,* and which
now fo long time I had with great
earneft

earneftnefs attended, and which laftly, by the account and calculation of the *Plannets*, I had moft diligently obferved, I found fo to be, yet could I never fore-fee that it muft happen under fo grievous and perilous conditions. For whereas I before imagined that to be a well-come, and acceptable Gueft, I needed only be ready to appear at the Wedding; I was now directed to Divine *Providence*, of which until this time I was never certain. I alfo found by my felf, the more I *examined* my felf, that in my Head there was nothing but *grofs* mif-underftanding, and blindnefs in myfterious things, fo that I was not able to comprehend even thofe things which lay *under* my Feet, and which I daily converfed with, much lefs that I fhould be born to the fearching out, and underftanding of the Secrets of Nature; fince in my opinion Nature might every where find a more *vertuou* Difciple, to whom to intruft her precious, though temporary, and changeable Treafures. I found alfo that my bodily behaviour, and outward good Converfation, and *Brotherly Love* toward my Neighbour, was

Requifita in hofpitibus Secundum.7. Pondera.

Electio incerta.

2

Infcitia Ignorantia Cæcitas mentis

3.

4.

Natura Secreta.

5.
6.

Maxima affectio

A 4   not

not duly purged and cleansed; Moreover the tickling of the Flesh manifest-
ed it self, whose affection was bent only to Pomp and Bravery, and Worldly
Pride, and not to the good of mankind ;
And I was always contriving how by
this art I might in a short time abun-
dantly increase my profit and advantage, rear up stately Palaces, make
my self an everlasting Name in the
World, and other the like *Carnal* de-
signs. But the obscure Words concerning the *Three Temples* did particularly afflict me, which I was not able
to make out by any after-Speculation,
and perhaps should not yet, had they
not been wonderfully revealed to me.
Thus sticking betwixt Hope and Fear,
examining my self again and again,
and finding only my own Frailty and
Impotency, not being in any wise able
to succour my self, and exceedingly
amazed at the fore-mentioned threat-
ning ; at length I betook my self to
my usual and most secure course ; after I had finished my earnest and most
fervent *Prayer*, I laid me down in my
Bed, that so perchance my good *Angel*
by the Divine permission might appear

Preces.

pear, and (as it had fometimes *formerly*
happened) inftruct me in this doubtful affair, which to the praife of God,
my own good, and my Neighbours
faithful and hearty warning and a-
mendment did now likewife fall out.
For I was yet fcarce fallen afleep, when
me-thought, I, together with a *number-*
lefs multitude of men lay fettered with
great Chains in a *dark Dungeon*, wherein without the leaft glimps of Light,
we fwarmed like Bees one over another, and thus rendred each others
affliction more grievous. But although
neither I, nor any of the reft could *fee*
one jot ; yet I continually heard one
heaving himfelf *above* the other, when
his Chains or Fetters were become ever
fo little lighter, though none of us
had much reafon to fhove up the o-
ther, fince we were all *Captive Wretches.*
Now as I with the reft had continued
a good while in this affliction, and each
was ftill reproaching the other with
his *blindnefs* and *captivity*, at length we
heard many *Trumpets* founding together, and Kettle-Drums beating fo
artificially thereto, that it even revived and rejoyced us in our Calamity.
During

Vifio per-
fomnium.

Tu ris Cæ-
citas.

During this Noise the *cover* of the Dungeon was from above lifted up, and a little *light* let down unto us. Then first might truly have been difcerned the buftle we kept, for all went pefle, mefle, and he who perchance had too much *heaved* up himfelf, was forced down again under the others Feet. In brief, each one ftrove to be *uppermoft*, neither did I my felf linger, but with my weighty Fetters flipt up from under the reft, and then heaved my felf upon a *Stone*, which I laid hold of; howbeit, I was feveral times caught at by others, from whom yet as well as I might, with Hands and Feet I ftill guarded my felf. For we imagined no other but that we fhould all be fet at *Liberty*, which yet fell out quite otherwife. For after the Nobles, who looked upon us from above through the Hole, had a while recreated themfelves with this our ftrugling and lamenting, a certain *hoary-headed Ancient* Man called to us to be quiet, and having fcarce obtained it, began (as I ftill remember) thus to fay on.

If

Illuftratio.

Lapis Præfidis.

Magifter Carceris.

If wretched Mankind would forbear
  Themselves so so uphold,
Then sure on them much good confer,
  My righteous Mother would :
But since the same will not insue,
They must in Care and Sorrow rue,
  And still in Prison lie.
Howbeit, my dear Mother will
  Their Follies over-see,
Her choicest Goods permitting still
  Too much in th' Light to be.
Though very rarely it may seem
That they may still keep some esteem,
Which else would pass for Forgery.
Wherefore in honour of the Feast
  We this day solemnize,
That so her Grace may be increast,
  A good deed she'l devise.
For now a Cord shall be let down,
And whosoe'er can hang thereon,
  Shall freely be releast.

*Vide S.
Bernhard.
Serm. 3. de
7. fragmen-
tis.*

He had scare done speaking, when
an Antient *Matron* commanded her Servants to let down the Cord *seven times*
into the Dungeon, and draw up whosoever could hang upon it. Good God!
that I could sufficiently describe the
                                hurry

*Magistra
restis.
Septies.*

hurry and difquiet that then arofe amongft us; For every one ftrove to get to the Cord, and yet only hindred each other. But after feven Minutes a fign was given by a little Bell, where-upon at the *firft* *Pull* the Servants drew up *four*. At that time I could not come near the Cord by much, having (as is before-mentioned) to my huge mif-fourtune, betaken my felf to a *Stone* at the Wall of the *Dungeon*, and thereby was difabled to get to the Cord which defcended in the middle. The Cord was let down the fecond time, but divers, becaufe their Chains were too *heavy*, and their Hands too *tender*, could not keep their hold on the Cord, but with themfelves beat down *many another*, who elfe perhaps might have held faft enough; Nay, many an one was forcably *pulled* off by another, who yet could not himfelf get at it; fo mutually *envious* were we even in this our great mifery. But they of all others moft moved my Compaffion, whofe weight was fo heavy, that they tore their very hands from their Bodies, and yet could not get up. Thus it came to pafs that at thefe five times very

Prima vectura.
4.

Secunda.

very few were drawn up. For as foon
as the fign was given, the Servants
were fo nimble at the draught, that the
moſt part tumbled one upon another,
and the Cord, this time eſpecially, was
drawn up very *empty*. Whereupon the
greateſt part, and even I my. felf, de-
ſpaired of Redemption, and called upon *God* that he would have pitty on us,
and (if poſſible) deliver us out of this
obſcurity, who alfo then, heard fome
of us : For when the Cord came down
the fixth time, fome of them hung   Sexta.
themfelves faſt upon it ; and whilſt in
the drawing up, the Cord fwung from
one fide to the other, it (perhaps by
the will of God) came to me, which I
fuddainly catching, got uppermoſt a-
bove all the reſt, and fo at length beyond hope came out ; whereat I exceedingly rejoyced, fo that I perceived not
the *Wound*, which in the drawing up I   Vulnus ex-
received on my *Head* by a fharp Stone,   turro Cæci-
till I with the reſt who were releaſed   tatis
(as was always before done) was fain,
to help at the feventh and laſt pull, at   Septima.
which time through ſtraining, the *Blood*
ran down all over my Cloathes, which
I neverthelefs for joy regarded not.
Now

Now when the last draught whereon
the most of all hung, was finished;
The Matron caused the Cord to be laid
Magistræ away, and willed her aged Son (at
filius. which I much wondred) to declare her
Resolution to the rest of the Prisoners;
who after he had a little bethought himself spoke, thus unto them.

    Ye Children dear
     All present here,
What is but now compleat and done,
Was long before resolved on:
What er'r my Mother of great Grace
To each on both sides here hath shown,
May never Discontent mis-place;
The joyful time is drawing on,
When every one shall equal be,
None Wealthy, none in Penury.
Who er'e receiveth great Commands
Hath work enough to fill his Hands.
Who er'r with much hath trusted been,
'Tis well if he may save his Skin,
Wherefore your Lamentations cease,
What is't to waite for some few days;

As soon as he had finished these
Words, the Cover was again put to
and locked down, and the Trumpets
                  and

and Kettle-Drums began afresh, yet could not the noise thereof be so loud, but that the bitter Lamentation of the Prisoners which arose in the Dungeon was heard above all, which soon also caused my Eyes to *run-over*. Presently after the Antient Matron, together with her Son sate down upon seats before prepared, and commanded the *Redeemed* should be told. Now as soon as she understood the number, and had written it down in a Gold-yellow Tablet, she demanded every ones Name, which were also written down by a little page; having viewed us all, one after another, she sighed, and spoke to her Son, so as I could well hear her, " Ah how hartily am I grieved for the " poor Men in the Dungeon! I would " to God I durst release them all, whereunto her Son replyed; ' It is ' Mother thus ordained of God, against ' whom we may not contend. In case ' we all of us were Lords, and possessed ' all the Goods upon Earth, and were ' seated at Table, who would there ' then be to be bring up the Service? whereupon his Mother held her peace, but soon after she said ; " Well, however

Magistra recenset vectos.

Secretarius.

Cur non omnes eveti.

"ever, let thefe be freed from their
"Fetters; whichwas likewife prefently
done, and I, except a few was the laft;
Gratitudo Auctoris e-vecti. yet could I not refrain, but (though I
ftill looked upon the reft; bowed my
felf before the Antient Matron, and
thanked God that through her, had
gracioufly and fatherly vouchfafed to
bring me out of fuch Darknefs into the
Light: After me the reft did likewife,
to the fatisfaction of the Matron. Laft-
Nummus Aureus. ly, to every one was given a piece of
Gold for a Remembrance, and to fpend
☉ by the way, on the one fide whereof
was ftamped the rifing Sun, on the
other (as I remember) thefe three Letters, *D L S*; And therewith every
Deus Lux Solis vel Deo laus Semp. one had Licenfe to depart, and was
fent to his own Bufinefs with this annex-
Mandatum Taciur ed Intimation, *That WE to the Glory of
God fhould benefit our Neighbours, and
referve in filence what we had been intrufted
with,* which we alfo promifed to do,
and fo departed one from another;
But in regard of the Wounds which
the Fetters had caufed me, I could not
well go forward, but halted on both
Feet, which the Matron prefently
efpying, laughing at it, and calling
me

me again to her faid thus to me, My Son, *Difceffus Au-*
let not this defeft afflift thee, but call *toris.*
to mind thy *Infirmities*, and therewith
thank God who hath permitted thee
even in this World, and in the ftate of
thy imperfeftion to come into fo *high*
a light, and keep thefe wounds for my *Vulnus et*
fake. Whereupon the Trumpets began *compedibus.*
again to found, which fo affrighted me
that I *awoke*, and then firft perceived *Expergefa-*
that it was onely a *Dream*, which yet *ctio.*
was fo ftrongly impreffed upon my ima-
gination, that I was ftill perpetually
troubled about it, and me thought I was
yet fenfible of the wounds on my Feet.
Howbeit, by all thefe things I well un- *Solatium.*
derftood that God had vouchfafed that
I fhould be prefent at this *myfterious and*
hidden Wedding ; wherefore with *Child-*
like confidence I returned thanks to his
Divine Majefty, & befought him; that he *Precatio.*
would further preferve me in his fear,
that he would daily fill my Heart with
Wifdom and Underftanding, and at
length gracioufly (without my defert)
conduft me to the defired end. Here- *Præparatio*
upon I prepared my felf for the *way*, *ad iter.*
put on my *white* linnen Coat, girded
my Loyns, with a *Blood-red* Ribbon
bound crofs-ways over my Shoulder:

B   In

Inm y Hat I ſtuck *four red* Roſes, that I might the ſooner by this Token be taken notice of amongſt the throng. For food I took *Bread*, Salt, and Water, which by the counſel of an underſtanding perſon I had at certain times uſed, not without profit, in the like occurrences. But before I parted from my *Cottage*, I firſt in this my dreſs, and wedding Garment, fell down upon my *Knees*, and beſought *God*, that in caſe ſuch a thing were, he would vouchſafe me a good iſſue. And thereupon in the preſence of God I made a vow, that if any thing through his grace ſhould be revealed unto me, I would employ it neither to my *own* honour nor authority in the World, but to the ſpreading of his *Name*, and the ſervice of my *Neighbour*. And with this vow, and good hope I departed out of my Cell with joy.

Votum.

The

The Second Day.

I was hardly got out of my Cell into a *Forreſt*, when me thought that the whole *Heaven* and all the Elements had already trimmed themſelves againſt this *Wedding*. For even the Birds in my opinion chanted more pleaſantly then before, and the young Fawns skipped ſo merrily, that they rejoyced my *old Heart*, and moved me to ſing : wherefore with a loud Voice I thus began : *Tripodium Creaturarum ob nuptias.*

With mirth thou pretty Bird rejoice,
*   Thy Maker's praiſe in-hanced.*
Lift up thy ſhrill and pleaſant Voice,
*   Thy God is high advanced.*
Thy food before he did provide,
*   And gives it in a fitting ſide,*
*   Therewith be thou ſufficed.*
Why ſhould'ſt thou now unpleaſant be,
*   Thy wrath againſt God venting ?*
That he a little Bird made thee,
*   Thy ſilly head tormenting ?*
Becauſe he made thee not a Man,
O peace, he hath well thought thereon.
*   Therewith be thou ſufficed.*

What

What is't I'd have poor earthly worm,
By God (as 'twere) inditing,
That I should thus 'gainst Heaven storm
To force great arts by fighting?
God will out-braved be by none,
Who's good for naught, may hence be gone,
O man b' herewith sufficed.
That he no Cæsar hath thee fram'd,
To pine therefore 'tis needless
His Name perhaps thou hadst defam'd
Whereof he was not heedless.
Most clear and bright Gods eyes do shine,
He pierces to thy heart within,
And cannot be deceived.

This fang I now from the bottom of my Heart throughout the whole Forreſt, *Per Sylvam.* fo that it refounded from all parts, and *In Campum.* the Hills repeated my laſt words, until at length I efpyed a curious *green* Heath, whither I betook my-felf out of the *Forreſt*. Upon this Heath ftood *3. Cedri.* three lovely tall *Cedars,* which by rea- *3. Templa.* fon of their *breadth* afforded an excellent and defired *ſhade,* whereat I greatly rejoyced ; for although I had not hitherto gone far, yet my earneſt longing made me very faint, whereupon I haſted to the Trees to reſt a little under them,

but

but as foon as I came fomewhat nigher, I efpyed a *Tablet* faftned to one of them, on which (as afterwards I read) in curious Letters the following words were written :

Tabella Mercurialis.
1. ☿

Hofpes falve : fi quid tibi forfitan de nuptijs *Regis* auditum, Verba hæc perpende. *Quatuor viarum* optionem per nos tibi *Sponfus* offert, per quas omnes, modo non in devias delabaris, ad Regiam ejus aulam pervenire poffis. Prima brevis eft, fed periculofa, et quæ te in varios *fcopulos* deducet, ex quibus vix te expedire licebit. Altera *longior*, quæ circumducet te, non abducet, *plana* eft et *facilis*, fi te *Magnetis* auxilio neque ad dex-

1.

2.

B 3 trum

trum , neque finiftrum ab-
duci patiaris. Tertia vere
Regia eft, quæ per varias Regis noftri delicias et fpecta-
cula viam tibi reddet jucun-
dam. Sed quod vix millefi-
mo hactenus obtigit. Per
quartam *nemini hominum* licebit ad Regiam pervenire, ut-
pote quæ confumens et non
nifi corporibus *incorruptibili-*
bus conveniens eft. Elige nunc
ex tribus quam velis, et in ea
conftans permane. Scito au-
tem quamcunque ingreffus
fueris, ab iinmutabili *fato* tibi
ita *deftinatum*, nec nifi cum
maximo vitæ periculo regre-
di fas effe. Hæc funt quæ te
fcivifte voluimus; fed heus
cave

cave ignores, quanto cum *peri-*
culo te huic viæ commiferis,
nam fi te vel minimi *delicti*
contra Regis noftri leges nofti
obnoxium, quæfo dum adhuc
licet per eandem viam qua
accelfifti domum te confer
quam citiffime.

Now as foon as I had read this Writing, all my joy was near vanifhed again,
and I who before Sang merrily, began
now inwardly to Lament. For although I faw all the *three ways* before
me, and nnderftood that hence forward
it was vouchfafed me, to make choice
of one of them ; yet it troubled me
that in cafe I went the ftony and *rocky*
way, I might get a miferable and deadly
fall, or taking the *long* one, I might wan-
der *out* of it through *by-ways*, or be
otherway's detained in the great Journey. Neither durft I hope, that I a-
mongft thoufands fhould be the very
He, who fhould choofe the *Royal* way.
I faw likewife the *Fourth* before me,
but it was fo invironed with *Fire* and

Exha-

Exhalations, that I durſt not (by *much*)
draw near it, and therefore again and
again conſidered, whether I ſhould return back, or take any of the ways before me. I well weighed my own *un-*
worthineſs, but the Dream ſtill comforted me, that I was delivered out of
the Tower, and yet I durſt not confi-
dently rely upon a Dream; whereupon I was ſo variouſly perplexed, that
for very great wearineſs, hunger and
thirſt ſeiſed me, whereupon I preſently drew out my *Bread*, cut a ſlice of
it, which a ſnow-white *Dove* of whom
I was not aware, ſitting upon the Tree,
eſpyed and therewith (perhaps accord·
ing to her wonted manner) came down,
and betook her ſelf very familiarly to
me, to whom I willingly imparted my
food, which ſhe received, and ſo with
her prettineſs did again a little refreſh
me. But as ſoon as her enemy a moſt
black Raven perceived it, he ſtreight
darted himſelf down upon the Dove,
and taking no notice of me, would
needs force away the Dove's meat, who
could no otherwiſe guard her ſelf but
by *flight*; whereupon they both *toge-*
ther flew toward the *South*, at which I
was ſo hugely incenſed and grieved,
that

Marginal notes:
Dubium.
Confirmatio.
Columba Alba arbori Mercuriali inſidens.
Corvus Niger.
Verſus Meridiem.

that without thinking what I did, I
made haſt after the filthy Raven, and
ſo againſt my will ran into *one* of the
forementioned ways a whole Fields
length; and thus the Raven being chaſed
away, and the Dove delivered, I then
firſt obſerved what I had inconſiderately
done, and that I was already. entred into a way, from which under peril of
great puniſhment I durſt not retire.
And through I had ſtill wherewith in
ſome meaſure to comfort my ſelf, yet
that which was worſt of all to me, was,
that I had *left my* Bag and *Bread* at the
Tree, and could never retrieve them:
For as ſoon as I turned my ſelf about, a
contrary wind was ſo ſtrong againſt me,
that it was ready to fell me. But if I.
went forward on my way, I perceived
no hinderance at all. From whence I
could eaſily conclude, that it would coſt
me my life, in caſe I ſhould ſet my ſelf
againſt the *Wind* ; wherefore I patient-
ly took up my croſs, got upon my feet,
and reſolved,ſince ſo it muſt be, I would
uſe my utmoſt endeavour to get to my
Journeys end before night. Now although many apparent *by-ways* ſhewed
themſelves, yet I ſtill proceeded with
my *Compaſs*, and would not budge one
ſtep

Autor in-
cidit in 2.
Viam in-
cogitanter.

Compaſius.

step from the Meridian Line ; howbeit the way was oftentimes so *rugged* and
unpassable,' that I was in no little doubt
of it. ' On this way I constantly thought
upon the *Dove* and *Raven*, and yet could
not search out the meaning, until at
length upon a high Hill' afar of I espy-
Diversorium ed a stately Portal,' to which not regarding how' far it was distant both
from me and the way I was in, I hasted,
Occasus ☉ because the Sun had already *hid* himself
under the *Hills*, and I (by far) could else-
where espy no abiding place, and this verily I ascribe only to God, who might
well have permitted me to go forward
in this way, and with-held my Eyes that
so I might have gazed beside this Gate.
To which(as was said) I now made mighty haste, and reached it by so much *Day-*
light, as to take a very competent view of
it. Now it was an exceeding *Royal beau-*
tiful Portal, whereon were carved a multitude of most *noble Figures* and Devices,
every one of which(as I afterwards learned)had its peculiar Signification; Above
Tabula in was fixed a pretty large Tablet, with
Scriptionis. these Words, *Procul hinc, procul ite pro-*
fani, and other things more, that I
was earnestly forbidden to relate. Now
Utitor. as soon as I was come under the Portal,
there

there ftreight ftepped forth one in a
Sky-coloured habit, whom I in friendly
manner faluted, which though he thankfully returned, yet he inftantly demand- Literæ con.
vocationis.
ed of me my Letter of Invitation.
O how glad was I that I had then
brought it with me! For how eafily might I have forgotten it (as it
alfo chanced to others) as he himfelf
told me ? I quickly prefented it, wherewith he was not only Satisfied, but (at
which I much wondred) fhewed me
abundance of refpect, faying, Come in
my *Brother*, an acceptable Gueft you
are to me ; and withal intreated me not
to with-hold my Name from him. Now
having replyed, that I was a Brother of
the *Red-Rofie Crofs*, he both wondred,
and feemed to rejoyce at it, and then Nomen Autoris.
proceeded thus, My Brother have you
nothing about you wherewith to pur-
chafe a Token ? I anfwered my ability
was fmall, but if he faw any thing
about me he had a mind to, it was
at his fervice. Now he having requefted of me my *Bottle* of Water, and I Emitor a-
qua Teffera.
granted it, he gives me a *golden Token*
whereon ftood no more but thefe two
Letters, *S. C.* intreating me that when Sanctitate
Conftantiæ
Sponfus
it ftood me in good ftead, I would
remem-

Charus.
Spes,
Charitas.

remember him. After which I asked him, how many were got in before me, which he also told me, and laitly out of meer Friendſhip gave me

Diploma.

a _ſealed Letter_ to the ſecond Porter. Now having lingered ſome time with him, the Night grew on : ·Whereupon a great _Beacon_ upon the Gate was immediately fired, that ſo if any were ſtill upon the way, he might make haſte thither. But the way where it finiſhed

The Caſtle.

at the Caſtle, was on both ſides incloſed with _Walls_, and planted with all ſorts of excellent Fruit-Trees, and ſtill on every third Tree on each ſide Lanthorns were hung up, wherein all the Candles were already lighted with a

Virgo Lucifera.

glorious Torch by a _beautiful Virgin_, habited in _Skye-colour_, which was ſo noble and Majeſtick a Spectacle, that I

The Lady Chamberlain or Controulor.

yet delayed ſomewhat _longer_ then was requiſite. But at length after ſufficient Information, and an advantageous Inſtruction, I friendly departed from the firſt Porter. On the way, though I would gladly have known what was written in my Letter, yet ſince I had no reaſon to miſtruſt the Porter, I forbare my purpoſe, and ſo went on the way, until I came likewiſe to the _ſecond Gate_,

which

which although it was very *like* the
other, yet was it adorned with Images & *Porta Secunda.*
myſtick ſignifications. In the affixed *Tablet*
ſtood *Date & dabitur vobis*. Under this *Tabella.*
Gate lay a terrible grim *Lyon* chain'd,
who as ſoon as he eſpi'd me aroſe & made *Cuſtos Leo.*
at me with great roaring : whereupon *2 Portitor.*
the ſecond Porter who lay upon a *Stone*
of Marble, awaked, and wiſhed me not
to be troubled or affrighted, and then
drove back the *Lion*, and having received the Letter which I with trembling reached him, he read it, and with
very great reſpect ſpake thus to me ;
Now well-come in Gods Näme unto me
the man whom of long time I would
gladly have ſeen. Mean while he alſo
drew out a *token*, and asked me whether I could purchaſe it ? But I having
nothing elſe left but my *Salt*, preſented *Teſſera*
it to him, which he thankfully accep- *empta ſale.*
ted. Upon this token again ſtood on- *Studio*
ly two Letters namely, *S. M.* Being *mereotis Sa!*
humor ſpon-
now juſt about to enter diſcourſe with *ſo mittendus*
him, it began to ring in the Caſtle, *Sal mine-*
ralis
whereupon the Porter counſelled me *Sal menſtru-*
to run apace, or elſe all the paines and *alis.*
labour I had hitherto taken would ſerve
to no purpoſe, for the *Lights* above
began already to be *extinguiſhed* ; whereupon

upon I difpatched with fuch hafte that I
heeded not the Porter, in fuch anguifh.
was I, and truly it was but neceffary,
for I could not run fo faft but that the
Virgin, after whom all the *lights* were
put out, was at my heels, and I fhould
never have found the way, had not fhe
with her Torch afforded me fome light;
I was more-over conftrained to enter
the very next to her, and the Gate was
fo fuddainly clap't to, that a part of my
coate was locked out, which I verily was
forced to leave behind me; for neither
I, nor they who ftood ready without
and called at the Gate could prevail
with the Porter to *open* it again, but
he delivered the Keys to the Virgin,
who took them with her into the Court.
Mean time I again furveyed the Gate,
which now appeared fo *rich*, as the
whole World could not equal it ; juft
by the Door were two Columns, on one
of them ftood a pleafant Figure with
this Infcription, *Congratuler*. The other
having its Countenance vailed was fad,
and beneath was written, *Candoleo*. In
brief, the Infcriptions and Figures
thereon, were fo dark and myfterious,
that the moft dextrous man upon Earth
could

Porta clau-
ditur.

Pyramides
Portæ.

could not have expounded them. But
all thefe (if God permit) I fhall e'er
long publifh and explain. Under this
Gate I was again to give my Name,
which was this laft time written down
in a little Vellum-Book, and immediately with the reft difpatched to the
Lord *Bridegroom.* Here it was where
I firft received the *true* Gueft-token,
which was fomewhat lefs than the former, but yet much heavier, upon this
ftood thefe Letters *S. P. N.* Befides
this, a new pair of Shoes were given
me, for the Floor of the Caftle was
laid with pure fhining Marble ; my *old*
Shoes I was to give away to one of the
Poor (whom I would) who fate in
throngs, howbeit in very good order,
under the Gate. I then beftowed them
on an old man : after which two Pages
with as many Torches, conducted me
into a litlte Room ; there they willed
me to fit down on a Form, which I did,
but they fticking their Torches in two
holes, made in the Pavement, departed
and left me, thus fitting alone. Soon
after I heard a noife, but faw nothing,
and it proved to be certain men who
ftumbled in upon me ; but fince I could
fee

Promiffura
Autetis.

Salus per
Naturam.
Sponfi præ-
fentandus
Nuptijs.

* Comes
puer.

see nothing, I was fain to suffer, and attend what they would do with me; but presently perceving them to be *Barbers*, I intreated them not to justle me so, for I was content to do whatever they desired, whereupon they quickly let me go, and so one of them (whom I could not yet see) fine and gently cut away the *Hair* round about from the *Crown of my Head*, but on my Fore-head, Ears and Eyes he permitted my *Icegrey* Locks to hang. In this first incounter (I must confess) I was ready to dispair, for inasmuch as some of them shoved me so forceably, and I could yet see nothing, I could think no other but that God for my *Curiosity* had suffered me to miscarry. Now these invisible Barbers carefully gathered up the *Hair* which was cut off, and carried it away with them. After which the *two* Pages entred again, and heartily laughed at me for being so terrified. But they had scarce spoken a few Words with me, when again a little Bell began to ring; which (as the Pages informed me) was to give notice for assembling; whereupon they willed me to rise, and through many Walks, Doors and wind

ing

Balneatores.

Capillus detonsus aſ- ſervatus.

Pueri bini.

ing Stairs lighted me into a ſpacious
Hall. In this Room was a great mul- Triclinium.
titude of gueſts, Emperors, Kings,
Princes, and Lords, Noble and Ignoble,
Rich, and Poor, and all ſorts of People, at which I hugely marviled, and
thought to my ſelf, ah, how groſs a
fool haſt thou been to ingage upon this
Journey with ſo much bitterneſs and
toil, when (behold) here are even thoſe
fellows whom thou well know'ſt, and
yet hadſt never any reaſon to *eſteem.*
They are now all *here*, and thou with
all thy Prayers and Supplications art
hardly got in at laſt. This and more
the Devil at that time injected, whom
I notwithſtanding (as well as I could)
directed to the iſſue. Mean time one
or other of my acquaintance here and
there ſpake to me: Oh Brother
Roſencreutz! art thou here too; yea,
(my Brethren) replyed I, the *Grace*
of God hath helped me in alſo; at
which they raiſed a mighty laughter,
looking upon it as ridiculous that there
ſhould be need of *God* in ſo ſlight an
occaſion. Now having demanded each Impietas
of them concerning his way, and found hoſpitum
that moſt were forced to clamber over non recta
via ingreſ-
ſorum.

C   the

the *Rocks*, certain Trumpets (none of which we yet faw) began to found to the Table, whereupon they all feated themfelves, every one as he judged himfelf above the reft; fo that for me and fome *other forry* Fellows there was hardly a *little Nook* left at the lowermoft Table. Prefently the two Pages entred, and one of them faid Grace in fo handfom and excellent a manner,

Quidam preces negligunt.

as rejoyced the very Heart in my Body. Howbeit, certain great Sr *John*'s made but little reckoning of them, but fleired and winked one at another, biting their Lips within their Hats, and ufing more the like unfeemly Geftures. After this

Commenfatio.

Meat was brought in, and albeit none could *be feen*, yet every thing was fo orderly managed, that it feemed to

Miniftri invifibiles.

me as if every Gueft had had his proper Attendant. Now my Artifts having fomewhat recruited themfelves, and the Wine having a little removed

Inebriatorum gloriatio vana.

fhame from their Hearts, they prefenrly began to vaunt and brag of their *Abilities*: One would prove this, another that, and commonly the moft *forry Idiots* made the loudeft noife. Ah, when I call to mind what *preternatural*

and

nd impossible enterprises I then heard,
I am still ready to vomit at it. In fine,
they never kept in their order, but
when ever one Rascal here, another
here, could insinuate himself in be-
ween the *Nobles*; Then pretended
hey the finishing of such *Adventures* as
neither *Sampson*, nor yet *Hercules* with
all their strength could ever have at-
chieved : This would discharge *Atlas*
of his burden; The other would again
draw forth the three-headed *Cerberus*
out of Hell : In brief, every man had
his own Prate, and yet the great *Lords*
were so simple that they believed their
pretences, and the Rogues so audacious,
that although one or other of them was
ere and there rapped over the Fin-
ers with a Knife, yet they flinched
not at it, but when any one perchance
ad filched a Gold-Chain, then would
all hazard for the like. I saw one who
eard the rustling of the Heavens :
The second could see *Plato's* Ideas :
a third could number *Democritus's* A-
oms. There were also not a few pre-
enders to the *perpetual motion*. Many
none (in my opinion) had good un-
erstanding, but assumed too to much to

him-

himſelf, to his own deſtruction. Laſt-
ly, there was one alſo who would
needs out of hand perſwade us that
he ſaw the *Servitors* who attended,
and would ſtill have purſued his Contention, had not one of thoſe inviſible

Miniſtri in-
viſibiles.

waiters reached him ſo handſom a cuſſ
upon his lying Muzzle, that not only
he, but many who were by him, became as mute as Mice. But it beſt of
all pleaſed me, that all thoſe, of whom
I had any *eſteem*, were very quiet in
their buſineſs, and made no loud cry
of it, but acknowledged themſelves to

Modeſtia
Proborum
hoſpitum.

be *miſ-underſtanding* men, to whom the
myſteries of Nature were too high, and
they themſelves much too ſmall. In this
Tumult I had almoſt curſed the day
wherein I came hither; For I could not
but with anguiſh behold that thoſe lewd
vain People were above at the Board,
but I in ſo ſorry a place could not, how
ever reſt in quiet, one of theſe Raſcal
ſcornfully reproaching me for a moth
Fool. Now I thought not that there
was yet one Gate *behind*, through which
we muſt paſs, but imagined I was during the whole Wedding, to continu
in this ſcorn, contempt and indignity
which

hich yet I had at no time deſerved, ither of the Lord Bride-groom or the ride; And therefore (in my opinion) e ſhould have done well to have ſought ut ſome other Fool to his Wedding han me. Behold, to ſuch *impatience* oth the Iniquity of this World reduce mple hearts. But this really was one art of my *Lameneſs*, whereof (as is efore mentioned) I dreamed. And nly this clamour the longer it laſted, e more it increaſed. For there were ready thoſe who boaſted of falſe and naginary *Viſions*, and would per- vade us of palpably lying Dreams. ow there ſate by me a very fine iet *Man*, who oftentimes diſcourſed f excellent matters, at length he ſaid, *ehold my Brother, if any one ſhould now me who were willing to inſtruct theſe ockiſh People in the right way, would he heard?* No, verily, replyed I. *The orld,* ſaid he, *is now reſolved (what- er comes on it) to be cheated, and can- t abide to give Ear to thoſe who intend good. Seeſt thou alſo that ſame Cocks- mb, with what whimſical Figures and oliſh Conceits he allures others to him. ere one makes Mouthes at the People with*

Impatien- tia ex ini- quitate ho- minum.

Aſſeſſor mo- deſtus.

Mundus vult decipi.

C 3   *unheard-*

unheard of Mysterious *Words. Yet believe me in this, the time is now coming when those shameful Vizards shall be plucked off, and all the World shall know what Vagabond Imposters were concealed behind them. Then perhaps that will be valued which at present is not esteemed.* Whilst he was thus speaking, and the clamour the longer it lasted, the worse it was, all on a suddain there began in the Hall

Musica.

such excellent and stately *Musick*, as all the days of my Life I never heard the like; whereupon every one held his peace, and attended what would become of it: Now there were in this Musick all sorts of *stringed* Instruments imaginable, which founded together in such harmony, that I forgot my self, and sate so unmovably, that those who sate by me were amazed at me, and this lasted near half an hour, wherein none of us spake one word, For as soon as ever any one was about

Multa, non attendenti- um.

to open his Mouth, he got an unexpected blow, neither knew he from whence it came: Me thought since we were not permitted to see the Musitians, I should have been glad to view only all the Instruments they made use of.

of. After half an hour this Muſick
ceaſed unexpectly, and we could neither ſee *nor* hear any thing further.
Preſently after, before the Door of
the Hall began a great *noiſe*, ſounding and beating of *Trumpets*, Shalms
and Kettle-Drums, alſo Maſter-like,
as if the Emperor of *Rome* had been
entring: whereupon the Door opened of it ſelf, and then the noiſe of the
Trumpets was ſo loud, that we were
hardly able to indure it. Mean while
(to my thinking) many thouſand *ſmall
Tapers*) came into the Hall, all which
of themſelves marched in ſo very exact
an order as altogether amazed us, till
at laſt the two fore mentioned Pages
with bright Torches, lighting in a
moſt beautiful *Virgin*, all drawn on a
glorioully gilded Triumphant Self-
moving Throne, entred the Hall. It
ſeemed to me ſhe was the very ſame
who before on the way kindled, and
put out the Lights, and that theſe her
Attendants were the very ſame whom
ſhe formerly placed at the Trees. She
was not now as before in Skye-colour,
but arrayed in a *ſnow-white* glittering
Robe, which ſparkled of pure Gold,

Facula ad lectum.

*Virgo Lucifera.
The Lady Chamberlain or Controular.*

Albedo.

C 4   and

and caſt ſuch a luſtre that we durſt not
ſteadily behold it. Both the Pages
were after the ſame manner habited
(albeit ſomewhat more ſlightly; as
ſoon as they were come into the middle
of the Hall, & were deſcended from the
Throne, all the ſmall Tapers made obei-
ſance before her: Whereupon we all
ſtood up from our Benches, yet every
one ſtaid in his own place. Now ſhe
having to us, and we again to her, ſhewed all Reſpect and Reverence; in a moſt
pleaſant Tone ſhe began thus to ſpeak;

The King my Lord moſt gracious,
Who now's not very far from us.
As alſo his moſt lovely Bride,
To him in troth and honour ti'd;
Already, with great joy indu'd,
Have your arrival hither view'd:
And do to every one, and all
Promiſe their Grace in ſpecial;
And from their very Hearts deſire,
You may it at the time acquire;
That ſo their future Nuptial joy
May mixed be with none's annoy.

Here-

Hereupon with all her ſmall Tapers ſhe again courteonſly bowed, and
preſently after began thus :

In th' Invitation writ, you know.   Propoſitio
That no man called was hereto   Actionis.
Who of God's rareſt gifts good ſtore
Had not received long before,
Adorned with all requiſit's,
As in ſuch caſes it befit's.
How though they cannot well conceit
That any man's ſo deſperate,
Under conditions ſo hard,
Here to intrude without regard ;
Unl-ſs he have been firſt of all,
Prepared for this Nuptial ;
And therefore in good hopes do dwell
That with all you it will be well :
Yet men are grown ſo bold, and rude,
Not weighing their ineptitude,
As ſtill to thruſt themſelves in place
Whereto none of them called was :
No Cocks-comb here himſelf may ſell,
No Raſcal in with others ſteal ;
For they reſolve without all let
A Wedding pure to celebrate.
So then the Artiſts for to weigh,   Probatio
Scales ſhall be fix't th' enſuing day ;   artificum.
                    Whereby

Whereby each one may lightly find
What he hath left at home behind:
If here be any of that Rout
Who have good cause themselves to doubt,
Let him pack quickly hence aside ;
For that in case he longer bide,
Of grace forelor'n, and quite undone
Betimes he must the Gantlet run :
If any now his Conscience gall,
He shall to night be left in th' Hall
And be again releas't by morn,
Yet so he hither ne'er return.
If any man have confidence,
He with his waiter may go hence,
Who shall him to his Chamber light
Where he may rest in peace to night ;
And there with praise awaite the Scale
Or else his Sleep may chance to faile.
The others here may take it well,
For who aim's 'bove what's possible,
'Twere better much he hence had pas't,
But of you all wee'l hope the best.

As soon as she had done speaking
this, she again made reverence, and
sprung chearfully into her Throne, after which the Trumpets began again
to sound, which yet was not of force to
take from many their grievous Sighs

So

So they again conducted her invisibly
away, but the most part of the small
Tapers remained in the Room, and still
one of them accompanied each of us.
In such perturbation 'tis not well possible to express what pensive Thoughts
and Gestures were amongst us. Yet
the most part resolved to await the
Scale, and in case things sorted not
well, to depart (as they hoped) in
peace. I had soon cast up my *reckoning*, *Autor humi-*
and being my Conscience convinced me*liat &.*
of all ignorance, and *unworthiness*, I
purposed to stay with the rest in the
Hall, and chose much rather to content my self with the Meal I had already taken, than to run the Risco of a
future repulse. Now after that every
one by his small Taper had severally
been conducted into a Chamber (each
as I since understood into a peculiar
one) There staid *nine* of us, and amongst
the rest he also, who *discoursed* with
me before at the Table. But although
our small Tapers left us not, yet soon
after within an hours time one of
the fore-mentioned Pages came in, and
bringing a great bundle of *Cords*
with him, first demanded of us whether

ther we had concluded to ſtay there, which when we had with Sighs affirm-ed, he *bound* each of us in a ſeveral place, and ſo went away with our ſmall Tapers, and left us poor Wretches *in Darkneſs.* Then firſt began ſome to perceive the imminent danger, and I my ſelf could not refrain Tears. For although we were not forbidden to ſpeak, yet *anguiſh* and *affliction* ſuffer-ed none of us to utter one word. For the Cords were ſo wonderfully made, yet none could cut them, muchleſs get them off his Feet : yet this comforted me, that ſtill the future gain, of many an one, who had now betaken himſelf to reſt, would prove very little to his ſatisfaction. But we by one only Nights Pennance might expiate all our preſumption : till at length in my ſor-rowful thoughts I fell aſleep ; during which I had a *Dream* ; Now although there be no great matter in it, yet I eſteem it not impertient to recount it : Me thought I was upon an *high Moun-tain*, and ſaw before me a great & large Valley, in this Valley were gather-ed together an unſpeakable *multitude* of People, each of which had at his

Head

Pernoctatio triſtis.

Somnium Typicum.

What will be the iſſue of the pro-

Head a *Thread*, by which he was hang- *batory beam.*
ed up towards Heaven, now one hung *e that*
high, another low, some stood even *climbs high*
quite upon the Earth. But in the Air *hath a great*
fall.
there flew up and down an *ancient* Man,
who had in his hand a pair of Sheers,
wherewith here he *cut* one's, and
there another's thread. Now he that.
was nigh the Earth was so much the
readier, & fall without noise, but when
it happened to one of the *high* ones, he
fell, so that the Earth quaked. To
some it came to pass that their Thread
was so stretched, that they came to the
Earth before the *Thread* was cut. I
took pleasure in this tumbling, and it
joyed me at the Heart, when he who
had *over-exalted* himself in the Air, of
his Wedding, got so shameful a fall,
that it carried even some of his Neighbours along with him. In like manner it
also rejoiced me, that he who had all this
while kept himself *near the Earth*, could
come down so fine and gently, that
even his next men perceived it not.
But being now in my highest fit of Jol-
lity, I was unawares jogged by one of
my fellow Captives, upon which I *Expergef.*
was awaked, and was very much dif-
contented

contented with him; Howbeit, I con-
fidered my Dream, and recounted it
to my Brother, who lay by me on the
other fide; who was not diffatisfied
with it, but hoped fome Comfort
might thereby be pretended. In fuch
difcourfe we fpent the remaining
part of the Night, and with longing
exfpected the Day.

The Third Day.

NOw as foon as the lovely day was
broken, and the *bright Sun*, having raifed himfelf above the Hills, had
again betaken himfelf, in the high
Heaven, to his appointed office; My
good Champions began to rife out of
their Beds, and leifurely to make themfelves ready unto the Inquifition.
Whereupon, one after another, they
Colloquium came again into the Hall, and giving
furgentium. us a good morrow, demanded how we
had Slept to Night; and having efpied
our Bonds, there were fome that re-
proved us for being fo cowardly, and
that we had not (much rather) as they,
hazarded

hazarded upon all adventures. Howbeit, some of them whose Hearts still
smote them made no loud cry of the
business. We excused our selves with
our *ignorance*, hoping we should now
soon be set at Liberty, and learn wit
by this disgrace? that they on the contrary had not yet altogether escaped, &
perhaps their greatest *danger* was still to
be expected : At length each one being
again assembled, the *Trumpets* began Cantus.
now again to sound & the Kettle Drums
to beat as formerly, and we then imagined no other but that the Bride-groom
was ready to present himself ; which
nevertheless was a huge mistake. For Virgo Lu-
it was again the *yesterday's Virgin* who cifera.
had arrayed her self all in *red Velvet*, The Lady
and girded her self with a *white Scarfe*. lain or Con-
Upon her Head she had a *green Wreath* troulor.
of Laurel, which hugely became her.
Her train was now no more of *small
Tapers*, but consisted of two hundred
Men in *Harnis*, who were all (like her)
cloathed in *red* and *white*. Now as
soon as they were alighted from the
Throne, she comes streight to us Pri-
ners, and after she had Saluted us,
she said in few words; That some of
you

you have been fenfible of your wretched condition is hugely pleafing to my
moft mighty Lord, and he is alfo re-

folved you fhall fare the better for it;
And having efpied me in my Habit, fhe
laughed and fpake, good lack! haft
thou *alfo* fubmitted thy felf to the Yoke,
I imagined thou wouldft have made thy
felf very fmug; with which Words fhe
caufed my Eyes to run over. After
which fhe commanded we fhould be
unbound, and cuppled together and
placed in a ftation where we might well
behold the Scales. For, faid fhe, it
may yet fare better with them, than
with the Prefumptious, who yet ftands
here at Liberty. Mean time the Scales

which were intirely of *Gold* were hung
up in the midft of the Hall; There was
alfo a little Table covered with red

Velvet, and *feven weights* placed thereon.
Firft of all ftood a pretty great one,
next four little ones; laftly, two great
ones feverally; And thefe Weights in
proportion to their bulk were fo *heavy,*
that no man can believe or comprehend

it: But each of the *Harnifed men* had
together with a naked Sword a *ftrong
rope*; Thefe fhe diftributed according

to

o the number of Weights into seven
ands, and out of every band chose
ne for their proper weight ; and then
gain sprung up into her high Throne.
Tow as soon as she had made her reve-
ence, with a very *Shrill* Tone she be-
an thus to speak :

Who int' a Painter's room does go
And nothing does of painting know,
Yet does in prating thereof, pride it ;
Shall be of all the World derided.

Who into th' Artists order goes,
And thereunto was never chose ;
Yet with pretence of skill does pride it ;
Shall be of all the World derided.

Who at a Wedding does appear,
And yet was ner'e intended there ;
Yet does in coming highly pride it ;
Shall be of all the World deried.

Who now into this Scale ascends,
The weights not proving his fast Friends,
And that it bounces so does ride it ;
Shall be of all the World derided.

As soon as the Virgin had done speak-
ng, one of the Pages commanded
ch one to place himself according
his order, and one after another to
ep in : which one of the *Emperors*

Ponderam
the Artifi-
ces.

i / Gelac,

D   made

made no scruple of, but first of all
bowed himself a little towards the
Virgin, and afterwards in all his stately Attire went up : where upon *each*
Captain laid in his weight; which (to
the wonder of all) he stood out. But
the *last* was too heavy for him, so that
forth he must ; and that with such anguish that (as it seemed to me) the Virgin her self had pitty on him, who also
beckned to her people to hold their
peace, yet was the good Emperor
bound and delivered over to the Sixth
band. Next him again came forth *another Emperor*, who stept hautily into
the Scale, and having a great *thick Book*
under his Gown, he imagined not to
fail ; But being scarce able to abide the
third weight, and being unmercifully
flung down, and his Book in that affrightment flipping from him, all the
Soldiers began to laugh, and he was
delivered up bound to the third band.
Thus it went also with some others of
the Emperors, who were all shamefully laughed at and captived. After these
comes forth a little *short Man* with a
curld brown Beard *an Emperor too*,
who after the usual reverence got up
                                        also

also, and held out so steadfastly, that
me thought, had there been more
weights ready, he would have out-
stood them; To whom the Virgin immediately arose, and bowed before
him, causing him to put on a Gown
of *red Velvet*, and at last reached him
a branch of *Lawrel*, having good store
of them upon her Throne, upon the
steps whereof she willed him to sit
down. Now how, after him it fared
with the rest of the Emperors, Kings
and Lords, would be too long to recount; but I cannot leave unmentioned
that few of those great *personages* held
out. Howbeit sundry *eminent vertues*
(beyond my hopes) were found in many. One could stand out this, the second
another, some two, some three, four
or five, but few could attain to the just
perfection; But every one who failed,
was miserably laughed at by the bands.
After the Inquisition had also passed
over the Gentry, the learned, and un-
learned, and the rest, and in each condition perhaps *one*, it may be, *two*, but
for the most part none; was found
perfect; it came at length to those
honest Gentlemen the vagabond *Chea-*

sers, and rascally *Lapidem Spiralansicum* makers, who were set upon the Scale with such scorn, that I my self for all my grief was ready to burst my Belly with laughing, neither could the very Prisoners themselves refrain. For the most part could not abide that severe trial, but with *Whips* and Scourges were jerked out of the Scale, and led to the other Prisoners, yet to a suiteable band. Thus of so great a throng so few remained, that I am ashamed to discover their number. Howbeit there were Persons of quality *also* amongst them, who notwithstanding were (like the rest) honoured with Velvet *Robes* and wreaths of Lawrel.

Nobiles nihilominus onantur.

The Inquisition being compleatly finished, and none but we poor coupled hounds standing aside; At length one of the Captains stepped forth, and said, Gratious Madam, if it please your Ladyship let these poor men, who *acknowledged* their mis-understanding, be set upon the Scale also without their incurring any danger of penalty, and only for recreation's sake, if perchance any thing that is right may be found

Proba Humilium.

amongst

amongſt them· In the firſt place I was in great perplexity, for in my an-guiſh this was my only comfort, that I was not to ſtand in ſuch ignominy, or to be laſhed out of the Scale. For I nothing doubted but that many of the Priſoners wiſhed that, they had ſtay'd ten Nights with us in the Hall. Yet ſince the Virgin conſented, ſo it muſt be, and we being untied were one af-ter another ſet up: Now although the moſt part miſcarried, yet they were neither laught at, nor ſcourged, but peaceably placed on one ſide. My Companion was the fifth, who held out bravely, whereupon all, but eſpecially the Captain who made the requeſt for us, applauded him, and the Virgin ſhewed him the uſual reſpect. After him again two more were diſpatched, in an inſtant. But I was the *eighth*; Now as ſoon as (with trembling) I ſtepped up, my Companion who alrea-dy ſat hy in his *Velvet*, looked friendly upon me, and the Virgin her ſelf ſmi-led a little. But for as much as I out-ſtayed *all the* Weights, the Virgin com-manded them to draw me up by force, wherefore three *men* moreover hung on

Socius Auto-ris.

Autor 8.

D 3   the

the otherside of the Beam, and yet could nothing prevail. Whereupon one of the Pages immediately stood up, and cryed out exceeding loud, *T.H.A.T's H E.* Upon which the other replyed, *Then let him gain his Liberty,* which the Virgin accorded; and being received with due Ceremonies. The choice was given me to release *one of* the Captives, whosoever I pleased; Whereupon I made no long deliberation, but elected the *first* Emperor whom I had long pittied, who was immediately set free, and with all respect seated amongst us. Now the last being set up, and the Weights proving too heavy for him, in the mean while the Virgin espied my *Rose,* which I had taken out of my Hat into my Hands, and thereupon presently by her Page graciously requested them of me, which I readily sent her. And so this first *Act* was finished about *ten* in the fore-noon. Whereupon the Trumpets began to sound again, which nevertheless we could not as yet see. Mean time the Bands were to step aside with their Prisoners, and expect the Judgment. After which a Council of the

seven

Margin notes:

That's he.

Probatissimus.

Liberat 1. Cæsarem.

Autor rosam suam donat Virgini.

Hora 10. Actus.

seven Captains and us was set, and the
business was propounded by the Virgin as
President, who desired each one to give
his opinion, how the Prisoners were
to be dealt with. The first opinion
was, That they should all be put to
Death, yet one more severely than another: namely those who had presump-
tuously intruded themselves contrary
to the Express conditions; others would
have them kept close prisoners! Both
which pleased neither the *President*, nor
me. At length by one of the Emperors
(the same whom I had freed) my Companion, and my self the affair was
brought to this point; That first of all
the principal *Lords* should with a be-
fitting respect be led out of the Castle;
others might be carried out somewhat
more scornfully. These should be
stripped, and caused to run out naked;
The fourth with Rods, Whips, or
Dogs, should be hunted out. Those
who the day before willingly surren-
dred themselves, might be suffered to
depart without any blame. And last of
all those Presumptuous ones, and they
who behaved themselves so unseemly at
Dinner the day before, should be pun-

ished

shed in *Body and Life* according to each
Mans demerit.   This opinion pleafed
the Virgin well, and obtained the upper hand.   There was moreover another Dinner vouchfafed them, which
they were foon acquainted with.   But
the Execution was deferred till twelve
at noon, Herewith the *Senate arofe*, and
the *Virgin* alfo, together with her Attendants returned to her ufual quarter.
But the uppermoft Table in the Room
was allotted to us, they requefling us to
take it in good part till the Bulinefs
were fully difpatched.   And then we
fhould be conducted to the *Lord Bride-*
groom and the *Bride*, with which we
were at prefent well content. Mean time
the Prifoners were again brought into
Frendum.   the Hall, and each Man feated according to his Quality ; they were likewife
enjoyned to behave themfelves fomewhat more civilly than they had done
the day before, which yet they needed
not to have been admonifhed, for (without this, they had already put up their
pipes.   And this I can boldly fay, not
with flattery, but in the love of truth,
that commonly thofe perfons who were
of the *higheft Rank*, beft underftood how
to

to behave themselves in so unexpected a misfortune. Their Treatment was but indifferent, yet with respect, neither could they yet see their *Attendants*, but to us they were visible, whereat I was exceeding joyful. Now although Fourtune had exalted us, yet we took not upon us more than the rest, advising them to be of good Cheer, the event would not be so ill. Now although they would gladly have understood the Sentence of us, yet we were so deeply obliged that none durst open his Mouth about it. Nevertheless we comforted them as well as we could, drinking with them to try if the Wine might make them any thing cheerfuller. Our Table was covered with *red V. I. vet*, beset with drinking-Cups of pure *Silver* and *Gold*; which the rest could not behold without amazement and very great anguish. But e're we had seated our selves, in came the two Pages, presenting every one, in the *Bridegroom's* behalf, the *Gold n Fleece* with a flying *Lyon*, requesting us to wear them at the Table, and as became us, to observe the Reputation and Dignity of the Order, which his Majesty had now vouch-

Ministri invisibiles, visibiles.

Probatio Exaltatio-

Remuneratio a Spe.

vouchfafed us, and fhould fuddenly be
ratified with futable Ceremonies. This
we received with profoundeft fubmif-
fion, promifing obediently to perform
whatfoever his Majefty fhould pleafe.
Befides thefe, the noble Page had a
Schedule, wherein we were fet down
in order. And for my part I fhould
not otherwife be defirous to conceal
my place, if perchance it might not be
interpreted to Pride in me, which yet
is exprefly againft the *fourth.* Weight.
Now becaufe our entertainment was
exceeding ftately, we demanded one
of the Pages, whether we might not
have leave to fend fome choice bit to
our Friends and Acquaintance, who
making no difficulty of it, every one
fent plentifully to his acquaintance by
the waiters, howbeit they faw none of
them; and forafmuch as they knew not
whence it came, I was my *felf* defirous
to carry fomewhat to one of them,
but as foon as I was rifen, one of the
Waiters was prefently at my Elbow,
faying, *He defired me to take friendly
marking, for in cafe one of the Pages had
feen it, it would have come to the King's
Ear, who would certainly have taken it
amifs*

Autori de-
negatur
communica-
tio erga re-
probos.

amiss of me? but since none had observed
it but himself, he purposed not to betray me,
but that I ought for the time to come to
have better regard to the dignity of the
order: With which words the Servant did really so astonish me, that for
a long time after I scarce moved upon
my Seat, yet I returned him Thanks
for his faithful warning, as well as in
haste and affrightment I was able.
Soon after the Drums began to beat
again; to which we were already ac-
customed: For we well knew it was
the *Virgin*, wherefore we prepared
our selves to receive her, who was now
coming in with her usual Train, upon
her high Seat, one of the Pages bear-   *Virgo Luci-*
ing before her a very tall Goblet of   *fera.*
Gold. And the other, a Patent in   *The Lady*
Parchment: Being how after a mar-   *Chamber-*
vellous *artificial* manner alighted from   *lain or Con-*
the Seat, she takes the Goblet from the   *troulor.*
Page, and presents the same in the
King's behalf, saying, *That it was brought*
us from his Majesty, and that in honour of   *Cali*
him we should cause it to go round. Upon   Obambulans
the cover of this Goblet stood *Fortune*
curiously cast in Gold, who had in her
Hand a *red flying* Ensign, for which
                                        cause

cauſe I drunk ſomewhat the more ſad-
ly,as having been but too well acquainted with Fortune's way-wardneſs. But
the Virgin as well as we, was adorned with the Golden *Fleece* and Lyon,
whence I obſerved, that perhaps ſhe
was the preſident of the Order. Wherefore we demanded of her how the Order might be named? ſhe anſwered,
That it was not yet ſeaſonable to diſcover it, till the affair with the Priſoners were diſpatched. And therefore their Eyes were ſtill held; and
what had hitherto happened to us, was
to them only for an Offence and Scan-
dal, although it were to be accounted
as nothing, in regard of the honour
that attended us. Hereupon ſhe began
to diſtinguiſh the *Patent* which the other
Page held into two different parts, out
of which about thus much was read
before the firſt company.

    That they ſhould confeſs that they had
too lightly given Credit to falſe fictitious
Books, had aſſumed too much to them-
ſelves, and ſo came into this Caſtle, albeit
they were never invited into it, and per-
haps the moſt part had preſented themſelves
with deſign to make their Markets here,

and

Ornatus Vir-
ginis

Rep obi
dividuntur.

Accuſatio
prius par-
tis.

and afterwards to live in the greater Pride *and Lordlinefs ; And thus one had fedu-ced another, and plunged him into this dif-grace and ignominy, wherefore they were defervedly to be foundly punifhed.* Affectibus Mundanis

Which they with great humility readily acknowledged, and gave their Hands upon it. After which a fevere check was given to the reft, much to this purpofe.

That they very well knew, and were in their Confeiences convinced, that they had forged falfe fictitious *Books, had befooled others, and cheated them, and thereby had diminifhed Regal dignity amongft all. They knew in like manner what ungodly deceitful* Figures *they had made ufe of, in fo much as they fpared not even the* Divine Trinity *, but accuftomed themfelves to cheat People all the Country over. It was alfo now as clear as* Day *with what Practices they had indeavoured to enfnare the true* Guefts, *and introduce the Ignorant : in like manner, that it was manifeft to all the* World, *that they* wallowed *in open Where-dom, Adultery, Gluttony, and other Uncleanneffes : All which was againft the ex-refs Orders of our Kingdom. In brief, they knew they had difparaged Kingly Ma-jefty,* Alterius partis.

jefty, even amongst the common fort, and
therefore they should confefs themfelves to
be manifeft convicted Vagabond-Chea-
ters, Knaves and Rafcals, whereby they
deferved to be cashiered from the company
of civil People, and feverely to be punished.

Confeffio
invita.

The good Artifts were loath to come
to this Confeffion, but inafmuch as not
only the Virgin her felf threatned, and
fware their death; but the other party
alfo vehemently raged at them, and
unanimously cryed out, that they had
moft wickedly feduced them out of
the Light: They at length, to prevent
a huge misfortune, confeffed the fame
with dolour, and yet withal alledged
that what had herein happened was rot
to be animadverted upon them in the

Excufatio

worft fenfe. For in as much as the
Lords were abfolutely refolved to get
into the Caftle, and had promifed great
fums of Money to that effect, each one
had ufed all Craft to feize upon fome-
thing, and fo things were brought to
that pafs, as was now manifeft before
their Eyes. But that it fucceeded not,
"They in their opinion had dif-deferved no
"more than the Lords themfelves; As
"who fhould have had fo much under-
ftandnig

tanding as to confider that in cafe
ny one had been fure of getting in,
e would not, in fo great Peril, for the
ike of a flight gain, have clambered
ver the Wall with them. Their
oks alfo *fold fo mightily*, that who-
r had no other mean to maintain
ifelf, was fain to ingage in fuch a
ifenage. They hoped moreover,
t if a right Judgment were made,
y fhould be found no way to have
carried, as having behaved them-
es towards the Lords, as became
vants, upon their *earneft entreaty.*
: anfwer was made them, that his Refutatio
yal Majefty had determined to pu:
1 all, and every man, albeit one
re feverely than another. For al-
ugh what had been alledged by
m was partly true, and *therefore the*
ds fhould not wholly be indulged, yet
y had good reafon to prepare them-
res for Death, who had fo prefump-
ufly obtruded themfelves, and per-
is feduced the more ignorant againft
ir will; As likewife they who with
e Books had violated Royal Majefty,
the fame might be evinced out of
ir *very Writings* and Books.

Here-

Hereupon many began moſt pitteouſly to lament, cry, weep, intreat, and proſtrate themſelves, all which notwithſtanding could avail them nothing, and I much marvelled how the Virgin could be ſo reſolute, when yet their miſery cauſed *our Eyes* to run over, and moved our Compaſſion (although the moſt part of them had procured us much trouble, and vexation) For ſhe preſently diſpatched her Page, who brought with him all the *Curiaſſiers* which had this day been appointed at the Scales, who were commanded each of them to take his own to him, and in an orderly Proceſſion, ſo as ſtill each Curiaſſier ſhould go with one of the *Priſoners*, to conduct them into her great Garden. At which time each one ſo exactly recogniſed his own Man, that I marvelled at it. Leave alſo was likewiſe given to my yeſterday *Companions* to go out into the Garden unbound, and to be preſent at the Execution of the Sentence. Now as ſoon as every Man was come forth, the Virgin mounted up into her *High Throne*, requeſting us to ſit down upon the Steps, and to appear at the Judgment, which we refuſed

not

Dolor de ſententia.

Executio Sententiarum.

Spectatores.

not, but left all ſtanding upon the Table (except the Goblet, which the Virgin committed to the Pages keeping)
and went forth in our Robes upon the
Throne, which of it ſelf *moved* ſo gently as if we had paſſed in the Air, till in
this manner we came into the *Garden*,
where we aroſe altogether. This Garden was not extraordinary curious, only it pleaſed me that the Trees were
planted in ſo good order. Beſides there
ran in it a moſt coſtly *Fountain*, adorned with wonderful Figures and Inſcrip-
tions, and ſtrange Characters, (which
God willing I ſhall mention in a future
Book) In this Garden was raiſed a
wooden Scaffold, hung about with curiouſly painted figured Coverlets. Now
there were four *Galleries* made one over
another, the firſt was more glorious
than any of the reſt, and therefore
covered with a *white-Taffa Curtain*, ſo
that at that time we could not perceive
who was behind it. The ſecond was
empty and uncovered. Again the two
laſt were covered with *red* and *blew Taf-*
fata. Now as ſoon as we were come
to the Scaffold, the Virgin bowed her
ſelf *down* to the ground, at which we

Hortus.

Author pro-
mittit alta
librum.

E   were

were mightily terrified: For we might
eafily guefs that the *King* and *Queen*
muft not be far off; Now we alfo having duely performed our Reverence,
The Virgin lead us up by the winding
Stairs into the fecond Gallery, where
fhe placed her felf uppermoft, and us in
our former order. But how the *Empe-*
ror whom I had releafed, behaved him-

Gratitudo
Cæfaris erga
liberatorem. felf towards me, both at this time, as
alfo before at the Table, I cannot,
without flander of wicked Tongues,
well relate. For he might well imagine
in what Anguifh and Sollicitude he now
fhould have been, in cafe he were at
prefent to attend the Judgment with
fuch ignominy, and that only through

Præcmifla. *me* he had now attained fuch Dignity
and Worthinefs. Mean time the Vir-
gin who firft of all brought me the Invitation, and whom hitherto I had never fince feen, ftepped in; Firft fhe
gave one blaft upon her Trumpet, and
then with a very loud Voice declared
the Sentence in this manner.

Oratio ad
reos. *The Kings Majefty my moft gracious*
Lord could from his heart wifh, that all
and every one here Affembled, had upon
his

his Majesties Invitation presented themselves so qualified, *as that they might* (*to
his honour*) *with greatest frequency have
adorned this his appointed Nuptial and joyful Feast*. But since *it hath otherwise
pleased Almighty God, his Majesty hath
not whereat to murmur, but must be forced,
contrary to his own Inclination, to abide by
the antient and laudable Constitutions of
this Kingdom*. But now, *that his Majesty's innate Clemency may be celebrated
over all the World, he hath thus far ab-
solutely dealt with his Council and Estates,
that the usual Sentence shall be considerably
lenified*. So that in *the first place he is willing to vouchsafe to* the Lords *and* Poten-
tates, *not only their lives intirely, but also freely and frankly to dismiss them;
friendly and courteously intreating your
Lordships not at all to take it in evil* part
*that you cannot be present at his Majesties
Feast of Honour*; But *to remember that
there is* notwithstanding more *imposed upon your Lordships by God Almighty* (who
*in the distribution of his Gifts hath an in-
comprehensible* Consideration) than *you
can duely and easily sustain. Neither is
your Reputation hereby prejudiced, although
you be rejected by this our Order, since we*

Sententia.
Magnatum.

E 2   con-

cannot at once all of us, do all things. But
for as much as your Lordships have been se-
duced by base Rascals, it shall not cn their
part, pass unrevenged. And furthermore
his Majesty resolveth shortly to communicate
with your Lordships a Catalogue of Here-
ticks or index Expurgatorius, that you
may henceforward be able with better judgment to discern between the Good and the
Evil. And because his Majesty e're long
also purposeth to rummage his Library, and
offer up the seductive Writings to Vulcan,
he friendly, humbly, and courteously in-
treats every one of your Lordships to put
the same in Execution with your own, whereby it is to be hoped that all evil and Mis-
chief may for the time to come be remedied.
And you are withal to be admonished, never henceforth so inconsiderately to covet an
entrance hither, least the former excuse of
Seducers be taken from you, and you fall
into Disgrace and Contempt with all Men.
In fine, for as much as the Estates of the
Land have still somewhat to demand of
your Lordships, his Majesty hopes that no
Man will think much to redeem himself
with a Chain or what else he hath about
him, and so in friendly manner to depart
from us, and through our safe conduct to
betake himself home again.   The

The others who stood not, at the first, *Sententia.*
third, *and* fourth *weight, his* Majesty **2.**
will not so lightly dismiss. But that they
also may now experience his Majesty's gen-
tleness, it is his Command, to strip them
stark naked, *and so send them forth.*

Those who in the second *and* fifth *weight*
were found too light, shall besides Stripping, **3.**
be noted with one, two or more Brand-
marks, according as each one was lighter,
or heavier.

They who were drawn up by the sixth *or*
seventh, *and not by the rest, shall be some-* **4.**
what more gratiously *dealt withal, and*
so forward. For unto every combination
there was a certain punishment ordained,
which were here too long to recount.

They who yesterday separated themselves **5.**
freely of their own accord, shall go out at
Liberty without any blame.

Finally, the convicted vagabond-Chea- **6.**
ters *who could move up none of the weights,*
shall as occasion serves, be punished in
Body *and* Life, *with the Sword, Halter.*
Water *and* Rods. *And such Execution of*
Judgment *shall be inviolably observed for*
an Example unto others.

Herewith our Virgin *broke* her Wand,
and the other who read the Sentence,
blowed her Trumpet, and ſtepped with
moſt profound Reverence towards thoſe
who ſtood behind the Curtain. But
here I cannot omit to diſcover ſomewhat to the Reader concerning the
number of our Priſoners; of whom
thoſe who weighed *one*, were *ſeven*; thoſe
who weighed *two*, were *twenty one*; they
who *three*, *thirty five*; they who *four*,
thirty five; thoſe who *five*, *twenty one*;
thoſe who *ſix*, *ſeven*; but he that came
to the *ſeventh*, and yet could not *well*
raiſe it; He, was only one, and indeed
the ſame whom I releaſed. Beſides, of
them who wholly failed there were many: But of thoſe who drew all the
weights from the ground, but few.
And theſe as they ſtood ſeverally before
us, ſo I diligently numbred, and noted
them down in my Table-Book; And it
is very admirable that amongſt all thoſe
who weighed any thing, none was equal
to another. For although amongſt thoſe
who weighed three, there were thirty
five, yet one of them weighed the firſt,
ſecond, and third, another the third,
fourth, and *fifth*, a thrid, the fifth,
ſixth,

fixth, and feventh and fo on. It is likewife very wonderful that amongft one hundred twenty fix who weighed any thing, none was equal to another ; And I would very willingly name them all, with each Mans weight, were it not as yet forbidden me. · But I hope it may hereafter be publifhed with the *Interpretation*.

Now this Judgment being read over, the Lords in the firft place were well fatisfied, becaufe in fuch feverity they durft not look for a mild fentence. For which caufe they gave more than they were defired, and each one redeemed himfelf with Chains, Jewels, Gold, Monies and other things, as much as they had about them ; and with reverence took leave. Now although the King's Servants were forbidden to jear any at his going away, yet fome unlucky Birds could not hold laughing, and certainly it was fufficiently ridiculous to fee them pack away with fuch fpeed, without once looking behind them. Some defired that the promifed *Catalogue* might with the firft be difpatched after them, and then they would take fuch order with their Books

Reorum mores.

Miniftrorum mores,

as

as should be pleasing to his Majesty ; which was again assured. At the Door was given to each of them out of a Cup a *Draught* of *FORGETFULNESS*, that so he might have no further memory of misfortune.

After these the *Voluntiers* departed, who because of their ingenuity were ſuffered to paſs, but yet ſo as never to return again in the ſame faſhion ; But if to them (as likewiſe to the others) any thing *further* were revealed, then they ſhould be well-come Gueſts.

Mean while others were ſtripping, in which alſo an inequality (according to each mans demerit) was obſerv'd. Some were ſent away naked, without other hurt.   Others were driven out with ſmall Bells. Some were ſcourged forth. In brief the puniſhments were ſo various, that I am not able to recount them all.   In the end it came to the laſt alſo with whom ſomewhat a longer time was ſpent, for whilſt ſome were hanging, ſome beheading, ſome forced to leap into the Water, and the reſt otherwiſe diſpatching, much time was conſumed.   Verily at this execution my Eyes ran over, not indeed in regard of the

the punifhment, which they otherwife
for their impudency well deferved,
but in contemplation of *humane blind-*
nefs, in that we are continually bufi-
ing our felves in that which ever fince
the firft Fall hath been hitherto *Scaled* Commifera-
tionis expo-
up to us. Thus the Garden which fo fitio.
lately was quite full, was foon emptied; fo that befides the Souldiers there
was not a man left. Now as foon ias
this was done, and filence had been kept
for the fpace of five minut's; There Entertain-
came forward a beautiful fnow-*white* ment at
Unicorn with a golden coller (having in Night.
Unicorna.
it certain Letters) about his neck: In
the fame place he bowed himfelf down
upon both his fore-feet, as if hereby he
had fhown honour to the Lyon, who Leo.
ftood fo immoveably upon the fountain, that I took him to be of ftone
or brafs, who immediately took the Machæra.
naked *Sword* which he bare in his Paw,
and brake it in the middle in two, the
pieces whereof to my thinking funk into the *Fountain* : after which he fo long
roared, until a *white-Dove* brought a Columba.
branch of *Olive* in her bill, which the
Lyon devoured in an inftant, and fo was
quieted. And fo the Unicorn returned
to

to his place with joy. Hereupon our
Virgin lead us down again by the winding ſtaires from the Scaffold, and ſo
we again made our reverence towards
Diſceſſus ab hoc aſtu. the Curtain. We were to waſh our
hands and heads in the Fountain, and
there a little while to wait in our order,
till the King through a certain ſecret
Gallery were again returned into his
Hall, and then we alſo with choice
Muſick, Pomp, State and pleaſant diſcourſe were conducted into our former
lodging: And this was done about four
in the afternoon. But that in the mean-
while the time might not ſeem too long
to us, the Virgin beſtowed on each of
us a noble *Page*, who were not only
richly habited, but alſo exceeding
learned, ſo that they could ſo aptly
diſcourſe upon all ſubjects, that we had
good reaſon to be aſhamed of our ſelves.
Diſceſſus virginis Lu-ciferæ. Theſe were commanded to lead us up
and down the Caſtle (yet but into cer-
tain places) and if poſſible, to *ſhorten*
the time according to our deſire. Mean
time the Virgin took leave with this
conſolation, that at Supper ſhe would
be with us again, and after that celebrate the Ceremonies of the hanging up
of

of the *Weights*, requesting that we would in patience waite till the next day, for on the morrow we must be presented to the King. She being thus departed from us, each of us did what best pleased him. One part viewed the excellent paintings, which they copied out for themselves, and considered also what the wonderful Characters might signifie. Others were fain to recruit themselves again with *meat* and drink. I indeed caused my Page to conduct me (together with my Companion) up and *down* the Castle, of which walk it will never repent me as long as I have a day to live. For besides many other glorious Antiquities, the Royal *Sepulcher* was also shewed me, by which I learned more than is extant in *all Books.* There in the same place stands also the glorious *Phænix* (of which two years since I published a particular small discourse) And am resolved (in case this my narration shall prove useful) to set forth several and peculiar Treatises, concerning the *Lyon*, *Eagle*, *Griffon*, *Falon* and other like, together with their Draughts and Inscriptions. It grieves me

Hospitum modi in delectamentis.

Autoris.

Libellus de Phænice.

me alfo for my other Conforts, that they neglected fuch pretious Treafures. And yet I cannot but think it was the fpecial will of God it fhould be fo. I indeed reaped the moft benefit by my Page, for according as each ones *genius* lay, fo he led his intrufted into the quarters and places which were pleafing to him. Now the *Kyes* hereunto belonging were committed to my Page, and therefore this good Fortune hapned to me before the reft ; For although he invited others to come in, yet they imagining fuch *Tombs* to be only in the Church-yard, thought they fhould well enough get thither, when ever any thing was to be feen there. Neither fhall thefe *Monuments* (as both of us copied and tranfcribed them) be *withheld* from my thankful Schollars. The other thing that was fhewed us two was the Noble *Library* as it was altogether before the *Reformation*. Of which (albeit it rejoyces my Heart as often as I call it to mind) I have fo much the lefs to fay, becaufe the *Catalogue* thereof is very fhortly to be publifhed. At the entry of this Room ftands a *great* Book, the like whereof I never faw, in which all the Figures, Rooms, Portals,

Ufus eorum quæ Autor vidit.

Bibliotheca.

tals, also all the Writings, Riddles and the like, to be seen in the whole Castle, are delineated. Now although we have made some promise concerning *this* also, yet at present I must contain my self, and first learn to know the World better. In every Book stands its *Author* painted; whereof (as I understood) many were to be *burnt*, that so even their memory may be blotted out from amongst the Righteous. Now having taken a full view hereof, and being scarce gotten forth, another *Page* came running to us, and having whispered somewhat in our Pages ear, he delivered up the *Kyes* to him, who immediately carried them up the winding Stairs; But our Page was very much out of *Countenance*, and we setting hard upon him with Intreaties, He declared to us that the *King's Maj·sty* would by no means permit that either of the two, namely the *Library* and *Sepulchers*, should be seen by any Man and therefore he besought us as we tendered his Life, to discover it to no Man, he having already utterly denyed it: Whereupon both of us stood hovering between Joy and Fear, yet it continued in silence, and no Man made further inquiry about it. Thus in both places we confumed three hours; which does not at all repent me. Now although it had already ftrucken *Seven*, yet nothing was hitherto given us to *eat*, howbeit our hunger was eafie to be abated by conftant *Revivings*, and I could be well content to faft all my Life long with fuch Entertainment. About this time the Curious *Fountains*, Mines, and all kind of Art-Shops, were alfo fhown us, of which there was none but furpaffed all our Arts, though they fhould all be melted into one Mafs. All their Chambers were built in *femi-circle*, that fo they might have before their Eyes the coftly Clock-work which was erected upon a fair Turret in the Center, and regulate themfelves according to the courfe of the *Planets*, which were to be feen on it in a glorious manner. And hence I could eafily conjecture wherein our *Artifts* failed, howbeit its none of my duty to inform them. At length I came into a fpacious Room (fhown indeed to the reft a great while before) in the middle whereof ftood a tereftrial Globe, whofe Diameter contained thirty Foot, albeit near half of it, except a little which was covered with the fteps.

was

[marginal notes:]

Faftidium pulfum egregijs fpectaculis.

Officinarum conftitutarum finis.

Globus terrenus.

was let into the Earth. Two Men might readily turn this Globe about with all its Furniture, so that more of it was never to be seen, but so much as was above the Horizon. Now although I could easily conceive that this was of some special use, yet could I not understand whereto those *Ringlets* of Gold (which were upon it in several places) served ; At which my Page laughed, and advised me to view them more narrowly. In brief, I found there *my native Country noted with Gold also*: Whereupon my Companion sought his, and found that so too. Now for as much as the same hapened in like manner to the rest who stood by, The Page told us of a certain that it was yesterday declared to the King, Majest'y by their old *Atlas* (so is the Astronomer named)that all the gilded points did exactly answer to their native Countries, according as had been shown of each of them. And therefore He also, as soon as he perceived that I *undervalued my self, and that nevertheless there stood a point upon my native Country,* moved one of the Captains to intreat for us, that we should be set upon the Scale (without our Peril)

ril) at all Adventures; Especially seeing *one of our Native Countries had a notable good Mark:* And truly it was not without cause that He, the Page who had the greatest power of all the rest, was bestowed on me. For this I then returned him thanks, and immediately looked more diligently upon my native Country, and found more over that besides the *Ringlet*, there were also certain delicate *streaks* upon it, which nevertheless I would not be thought to speak to my own praise or glory. I saw much more too upon this Globe than I am willing to discover. Let each Man take into consideration why every City produceth not a Philosopher. After this he lead us quite into the Globe, which was thus made ; On the Sea(there being a large square besides it) was a Tablet, whereon stood three Dedications, and the Author's name, which a Man might gently lift up and by a little joyned Board, go into the *Center*, which was capable of four Persons, being nothing but a round Board whereon we could sit and at ease by broad-daylight (it was now already dark) contemplate the Stars, to my thinking, they

Excellentia Patriæ Autoris.

Quid in Glob.

they were mere *Carbuncles* which glit-
tered in an agreeable order, and moved fo gallantly, that I had fcarce any
mind ever to go out again, as the Page
afterwards told the Virgin, with which
fhe often twitted me: For it was already Supper time, and I had fo much
amufed my felf in the Globe, that I
was almoft the laft at Table; wherefore
I made no longer delay, but having a-
gain put on my *Gown* (which I had before layd afide) and ftepping to the
Table, the waiters treated me with fo
much reverence and honour, that for
fhame I durft not look up, and fo unawars permitted the Virgin, who attended me on one fide, to ftand, which
fhe foon perceiving twitched me by the
Gown, and fo led me to the table to
fpeak any further concerning the
Mufick, or the reft of that magnificent
entertainment, I hold it needlefs both
becaufe it is not poffible fufficiently to
exprefs it, and I have above reported
it according to my power. In brief,
there was nothing there but Art and A-
mænity. Now after we had each to
other related our employment fince

*Reverentia
in convivio
exhibita
Auctoris.*

F   noon

noon (howbeit, not a word was fpoken
of the Library and Monuments) being already merry with the Wine,
the Virgin began thus: My Lords, I
have a great contention with one of my
Sifters: In our Chamber we have an
Eagle, Now we cherifh him with fuch
diligence, that each of us is difirous
to be the beft beloved, and upon that
fcore have many a Squabble. On a day
we concluded to go both together to
him, and toward whom he fhould fhew
himfelf moft friendly, hers fhould he
properly be; this we did, and I (as
commonly) bare in my hand a branch
of Lawrel; but my Sifter had none.
Now as foon as he efpyed us both, he
immediately gave my Sifter another
branch which he had in his Beak, and
offered at mine, which I gave him.
Now each of us hereupon imagined
her felf to be beft beloved of him;
which way am I to refolve my felf?
This modeft propofal of the Virgin
pleafed us all mighty well, and each one
would gladly have heard the Solution,
but in as much as they all looked upon
me, and defired to have the beginning
from

The Lady Chamber-lain or Con-trouler.

Perplexed Speeches, or intricate Queftions.

from me, my mind was so extreamly Autoris
propo-
griphus. confounded that I knew not what else to do with it but propound another in its stead, and therefore said Gracious Lady, your Ladyships question were easily to be resolved if one thing did not perplex me. I had two Compani-The Authors
counter-de-
mand. ons, both which loved me exceedingly; now they being doubtful which of them was most dear to me, concluded to run to me unawars, and that he whom I should then embrace should be the right ; this they did, yet one of them could not keep pace with the other, so he staid behind and wept, the other I embraced with amazement. Now when they had afterwards discovered the business to me, I knew not how to resolve my self, and have hitherto let it rest in this manner, until I may find some good advice herein. The Virgin wondered at it, and well observed where about I was, whereupon she re-plied, well then let us both be quit; and then desired the solution from the rest. But I had already made them wise. Wherefore the next began thus. 3 ploe 3. In the City where I live, a Virgin was lately condemned to death, but the

Judge

Judge being something pittiful towards her, caufed it to be proclaimed that if any Man defired to become the Virgins Champion, he fhould have free leave to do it. Now fhe had two Lovers, the one prefently made himfelf ready, and came into the lifts to expect his adverfary, afterwards the other alfo prefented himfelf, but coming fome-what too late, he refolved never-thelefs to fight, and willingly fuffer himfelf to be vanquifhed, that fo the Virgin's life might be preferved, which alfo fucceeded according. *Whereup-on each challenged her : Now my Lords inftruct me, to which of them of right be-longeth fhe ?* The Virgin could hold no longer, but faid, I thought to have gain-ed much information, and am my felf gotten into the Net, but yet would gladly hear whether there be any more behind ; yes, that there is, anfwered the third, a Stranger adventure hath not been yet recounted then that which happened to my felf. In my Youth I loved a worthy Maid : Now that this my love might attain its wifhed end, I was fain to make ufe of an ancient Ma-tron, who eafily brought me to her. Now

it

it happened that the Maid's Brethren came in upon us juft as we three were together, who were in fuch a rage that they would have taken my Life, but upon my vehement Supplication, they at length forced me to fwear to take *each of them for aYear,*to my wedded Wife.*Now tell me my Lords, fhould I take the old, or the young one firft?* We all laughed fufficiently at this riddle, and though fome of them muttered one to another thereupon, yet none would undertake to unfold it. Hereupon the fourth began. In a certain City there dwelt an honourable Lady, who was beloved of all, but efpecially by a young noble Man, who would needs be too importunate with her; at length fhe gave him this determination, that in cafe he would, in a cold Winter, lead her into a fair green Garden of Rofes, then he fhould obtain, but if not, he muft refolve never to fee her more. The noble Man travelled into all Countries to find fuch a Man as might perform this, till at length he lite upon a little old Man that promifed to do it for him, in cafe he would affure him of half his Eftate ; which he having confented to,

the

the other was as good as his word.
Whereupon he invited the forefaid
Lady home to his Garden, where contrary to her expectation fhe found all
things green, pleafant and warm, and
withal remembring her promife, fhe
only requefted that fhe might once
more return to her Lord, to whom
with Sighs and Tears fhe bewailed her
lamentable condition : But for as much
as he fufficiently perceived her faithful-
nefs, he difpatched her back to her Lo-
ver, who had fo dearly purchafed her,
that fhe might give him Satisfaction.
This Husband's integrity did fo mightily affect the noble man, that he thought
it a fin to touch fo honeft a Wife; fo
he fent her home again with honour to
her Lord. Now the little Man perceiving fuch Faith in both thefe, would
not, how poor foever he were, be the
leaft, but reftored the noble Man all
his Goods again, and went his way.
Now (my Lords) I know not which of
thefe perfons may have fhown the grea-
teft ingenuity ? Here our Tongues
were quite cut off. Neither would
the Virgin make any other reply, but
only that another fhould go on. Wherefore

fore the fifth, without delay, began. *psal.* 6.
My Lords, I defire not to make long
work; who hath the greater joy, he
that beholdeth what he loveth, or he
that only thinketh on it? He that beholdeth it, faid the Virgin; nay anfwered I; hereupon arofe a contest,
wherefore the fixth called out, My 7.
Lords I am to take a Wife; now I
have before me a maid, a married
Wife, and a Widdow; eafe me of
this doubt, and I will afterwards help
to order the reft. It goes well there,
replyed the feventh, where a man hath 8.
his choice, but with me the cafe is o-
therwife; in my youth I loved a fair
and vertuous Virgin from the bottom
of my Heart, and fhe me in like manner: howbeit becaufe of her Friends
denyal we could not come together in
wedlock: Whereupon fhe was married
to another, yet an honeft and difcreet
Perfon, who miintained her honourably and with affection, until fhe came
into the paines of Child-birth, which
went fo hard with her that all thought
fhe had been dead, fo with much ftate,
and great mourning fhe was interred.
Now I thought with my felf, during
her

her Life thou couldſt have no part in this Woman, but yet now dead as ſhe is thou mayſt embrace and Kiſs her ſufficiently ; whereupon I took my Servant with me, who dug her up by Night ; Now having opened the Coffin and locked her in my Arms, and feeling about her Heart, I found ſtill ſome little motion in it, which increaſed more and more from my warmth, till at laſt I perceived that ſhe was indeed ſtill alive ; wherefore I quietly bare her home; and after I had warmed her chilled Body with a coſtly Bath of Herbs, I committed her to my Mother until ſhe brought forth a fair Son, whom (as the Mother) I cauſed faithfully to be nurſed. After two days (ſhe being then in a mighty amazement) I diſcovered to her all the forepaſſed affair, requeſting her that for the time to come ſhe would live with me as a Wife, againſt which ſhe thus excepted, in caſe it ſhould be grievous to her Husband who had well and honourably maintained her. But if it could otherwiſe be, ſhe was the preſent obliged in love to one as well as the other. Now after two Months (being then to make a Journey elſewhere)

elfewhere) I invited her Husband as a
Gueft, and amongft other things demanded of him; whether if his deceafed
Wife fhould come home again, he
could be content to receive her, and he
affirming it with Tears and Lamentations, at length I brought him his Wife
together with his Son, and an account
of all the fore-paffed bufinefs, intreating him to ratifie with his confent my
fore-purpofed efpoufals. After a long
difpute he could not beat me from my
right, but was fain to leave me the
Wife. But ftill the conteft was about
the Son. Here the Virgin interrupted
him, and faid, It makes me wonder how
you could double the afflicted Mans
grief. How, anfwered he, was I not
then concerned? Upon this there arofe
a difpute amongft us, yet the moft part
affirmed that he had done but right.
Nay, faid he, I freely returned him
both his Wife and Son. Now tell me
(my Lords) was my honefty, or this
Man's joy the greater? Thefe words
had fo mightily cheared the Virgin that
(as if it had been for the fake of thefe
two) fhe caufed a health to go round.
After which the reft of the propofals
went

went on somewhat perplexedly, so
that I could not retain them all, yet
this comes to my mind, that one

6.   said, that a few years before he had
feen a Phyfitian, who bought a parcel
of Wood againft Winter, with which
he warmed himfelf all Winter long,
but as foon as the Spring returned he
fold the very fame Wood again, and fo
had the ufe of it for nothing; Here
muft needs be skill, faid the Virgin,
but the time is now paft. Yea, replyed
my Companion, who ever underftands
not how to refolve all the Riddles,
may give each Man notice of it by a
proper Meffenger, I conceive he will
not be denied. At this time they began to fay Grace, and we arofe altogether from the Table, rather fatisfied
and merry than glutted; and it were to
be wifhed that all *Invitations* and Feaft-
ings were thus to be kept. Having now
taken fome few turns up and down the
Hall again, the Virgin afked us whether

The Lady we defired to begin the Wedding.
Chamber-
lain Yes, faid one, noble and vertuous La-
virg. Lucif. dy; whereupon fhe privately difpatch-
Gratiofitas. ed a Page, and yet in the mean time
proceeded in difcourfe with us. In

brief

brief she was already become so fami-
liar with us, that I adventured and re-
queſted her Name· The Virgin ſmiled
't my Curioſity, but yet was not moved, but replyed, *My Name contains* Ænigma de
five and fifty, and yet hath only eight Let- Nomine.
ters, the third is the third part of the fifth,
which added to the ſixth will produce a
Number, whoſe root ſhall exceed the third
it ſelf by juſt the firſt, and it is the half
of the fourth. Now *the fifth and the ſe-*
venth are equal, the laſt and the firſt are
alſo equal, and make with the ſecond as
much as the ſixth hath, which contains juſt
four more than the third tripl'd. Now
tell me, my Lord, how am I called? The
anſwer was intricate enough to me, yet
I left not off ſo, but ſaid, noble and
vertuous Lady, may I not obtain one
only Letter? *Yea* (ſaid ſhe) *that may*
well be done. What then (replyed I a-
gain) may the ſeventh contain? *It con-* 60.
tains (ſaid ſhe) *as many as there are Lords* Sc.quot Virgines.
here. With this I was content,and eaſily
found her Name, at which ſhe was well Reddunter
pondera
pleaſed, with aſſurance that much *more* choro Vir-
ſhould yet be revealed to us. Mean ginum.
time certain Virgins had made themſelves ready, and came in with great
Cere-

2. Juvenos. Ceremony. Firſt of all two Youths carried Lights before them, one of them was of a jocond Countenance, ſprightly Eyes and gentile Proportion. The other lookt ſomething angerly, whatever he would have, muſt be, as I

4. Virgines. afterwards perceived. After them firſt followed four Virgins; one looked ſhame-facedly towards the Earth, very humble in Behaviour; The ſecond alſo was a modeſt, baſhful Virgin; The third, as ſhe entered the Room ſeemed amazed at ſomewhat, and as I underſtood, ſhe cannot well abide where there is too *much Mirth.* The fourth brought with her certain ſmall *wreaths,* thereby to manifeſt her Kindneſs and

2. Virgines Liberality. After theſe four came two which were ſomewhat more gloriouſly Apparelled; they ſaluted us courteouſly; One of them had a Gown of *Skye* coulour ſpangled with golden Stars; The others was *green,* beautified with red and white ſtripes. On their Heads they had thin flying *Tiffaties,* which did moſt becomingly adorn them. At laſt came one alone, who had

1. Virgo præ- on her head a *Coronet,* but rather looked up towards Heaven, than towards Earth.
ſtans.

..r h. We all thought it had been the
l.e Bride, but were much miftaken,
hough otherwife in Honour, Riches
.1d State fhe much furpaffed the *Bride* ; the Dutches.
.ind fhe afterwards ruled the whole
Wedding. Now on this occafion we
all followed our Virgin, and fell down
on our Knees, howbeit fhe fhewed her
feif extream humble, offering every one
her hand, and admonifhing us not to be
:oc much furprized at this, for this was
one of her fmalleft Bounties, but to lift up
our Eyes to our Creator, and learn here-
y to acknowledge his Omnipotency,
nd fo proceed in our enterprifed
courfe, employing this Grace to the
praife of God, and the good of Man.
In fum, her words were quite diffe-
nt from thofe of our *Virgin*, who
was fomewhat *more worldly.* They
pierced even through my Bones and
Marrow. *And thou*, faid fhe further to
r.. *haft received more than others, fee
.at thou alfo make a larger return.* This
.o me was a very ftrange Sermon ; for
as foon as we faw the Virgins with the
'.fick, we immagined we muft pre-
:ntly fall to Dancing, but that time
a: not as yet come. Now the Weights,
whereof

whereof mention hath been before
made, stood still in the same place,
wherefore the Queen (I yet knew not
who she was) commanded each Virgin
to take *up* one, but to our Virgin she
gave her own, which was the last and
greatest, and commanded us to follow
behind ; our Majesty was then somewhat abated, for I well observed that our
Virgin was but too good for us,&that we
were not so highly reputed as we ourselves were almost in part willing to
phantsie. So we went behind in our
order, and were brought into the first
Chamber, where our Virgin in the first
place hang up the *Queen*'s weight, during
which an excellent spiritual Hymn was
Sung ; there was nothing costly in this
Room save only certain curious little
Prayer Books which should never be
missing. In the midst was erected a
Pulpit, very convenient for Prayer.
where in the *Queen* kneeled down, about
her we were all fain to kneel and pray
after the Virgin, who read out of a Book,
That this Wedding might tend to the
Honour of God, and our own benefit
Afterwards we came into the second
Chamber, where the *first Virgin* hung
up

Ponderum repositio in locum suum.

the Dutches.

Reginæ habitatio.

the Dutches.

Supellex.

the Dutches.

p her weight alſo, and ſo forward till
ll the Ceremonies were finiſhed. Here·
ıpon the *Queen* again preſented her
Hand to every one, and departed
thence with her Virgin. Our Preſident ſtaied yet a while with us. But
becauſe it had been already two hours *Virgo Lucif.*
diſcedit
cubatum.
night, ſhe would no longer detain us ;
me thought ſhe was glad of our Company, yet ſhe bid us good night, and
wiſhed us quiet reſt, and ſo departed
friendly, although *unwillingly* from us.
Our Pages were well inſtructed in their *Puerorum*
comitum
Officium.
buſineſs, and therefore ſhewed every
Man his Chamber, and ſtayed alſo with
us in another Pallet, that in caſe we
wanted any thing we might make uſe of
them. My Chamber (of the reſt I am
not able to ſpeak) was royally furniſh- *Autoris*
thalamus.
ed with rare *Tapiſtries,* and hung about
with Paintings. But above all things
I delighted in my Page, who was ſo
excellently ſpoken, and experienced in
the *Arts,* that he yet ſpent me another
hour, and it was half an hour after three
when firſt I fell aſleep. And this indeed
was the firſt night that I ſlept in quiet,
and yet a ſcurvy Dream would not ſuf·
fer me to reſt ; For I was all the night
troubled

Somnium de portá difficili.

troubled with a *Door* which I could not get open, but at laſt I did it. With theſe phantaſies I paſſed the time, till at length towards day I awaked.

The fourth Day.

Autor long-iuſcule dor-miens ex-pergeſit.

I Still lay in my Bed, and leiſurely ſurvieghed all the noble Images and Figures up and down about my Chamber, during which on a ſudden I heard the *Muſick* of Coronets, as if they had been already in Proceſſion. My Page skipped out of the Bed as if he had been at his wits end, and looked more like one dead than living; In what caſe I then was, is eaſily immaginable, for, ſaid he, *The reſt are already preſented to the King* ; I knew not what elſe to do, but weep out-right, and Curſs my own ſloathfulneſs ; yet I dreſ-ſed my ſelf, but my Page was ready long before me, and ran out of the Chamber to ſee how affairs might yet ſtand. But he ſoon returned, and brought with him this joyful news,

that

that the time indeed was not yet past, *Jentaculo privatur.*
only I had over-*slept* my Breakfast, they
being unwilling to waken me because of
my Age ; But that now it was time for
me to go with him to the *Fountain* where
the most part were assembled ; With
this Consolation my Spirit returned a-
gain, wherefore I was soon ready with
my Habit, and went after the Page to
the *Fountain* in the afore-mentioned
Garden, where I found that the *Lyon*
instead of his Sword had a pretty large *Leonis Tabula.*
Tablet by him. Now having well
viewed it, I found that it was taken
out of the ancient Monuments, and
placed here for some especial Honour.
The Inscription was somewhat worn
out with age, and therefore I am mind-
ed to set it down here, as it is, and give
every one leave to consider it.

G HERMES

HERMES PRINCEPS.
POST TOT ILLATA
GENERI HUMANO DAMNA,
DEI CONSILIO:
ARTISQUE ADMINICULO,
MEDICINA SALUBRIS FACTUS
HEIC FLUO.

Bibat ex me qui poteſt: lavet, qui vult:
turbet qui audet:
BIBITE FRATRES, ET VIVITE.

⚛ 𝔇:XXIC☿ ﮞ

Scriptura facilis. This Writing might well be read and
underſtood, and may therefore fitly
be here placed, becauſe eaſier than any
of the reſt : Now after we had firſt
waſhed our ſelves out of the Fountain,
and every Man had taken a draught out
Potus. of an intirely Golden Cup, we were
once more again to follow the Virgin
into the Hall, and there put on new
Apparel,

Apparel, which was all of Cloth of *vestitar.*
Gold glorioufly fet out with Flowers.
There was alfo given to every one another Golden *Fleece*, which was fet about
with pretious Stones, and various
Workmanfhip according to the utmoft
skill of each Artificer. On it hung a
weighty Medal of Gold, whereon were
figured the *Sun* and *Moon* in oppofition;
but on the other fide ftood this Poefie,
The light of the Moon fhall be as the light
of the Sun, and the light of the Sun fhall
be feven times lighter than at prefent. But *Clinodia.*
our former Jewels were layed in a lit-
tle Casket, and committed to one of the
Waiters. After this the Virgin lead
us out in our order, where the Mufiti- *Mafici.*
ans waited ready at the door, all appa-
ralled in *red Velvet* with white Guards.
After which a *Door* (which I never faw *Acceffus*
open before) to the Royal winding- *ad Regis*
Stairs was unlocked; There the Vir- *Aulam.*
gin led us together with the Mufick, up
three hundred fixty five Stairs, there we
faw nothing but what was of extream
coftly and artificial Workmanfhip;
and ftill the further we went, the more
glorious ftill was the Furniture, until
at length at the top we came under a

Laboratorium arcuatum 60.Virgines. *painted* Arch, where the *sixty* Virgins attended us, all Richly Apparelled; Now as soon as they had bowed to us, and we as well as we could, had returned our reverence, our Musitians were dispatched away, who were fain to go down the winding-Stairs again, the Door being shut after them. After this a little Bell was tolled; then came in a beautiful Virgin who brought every one a wreath of Laurel; But our Virg. Lucif. Virgins had Branches given them: Mean while a Curtain was drawn up; Where I saw the *King* and *Queen* as they sate there in their Majesty, and had not the yesterday Queen so faithfully warned me, I should have forgotten my self, and have equalled this unspeak-
Regis & Reginæ gloria. able glory to Heaven. For besides that the Room glistered of meer Gold and pretious Stones; the *Queen's Robes* were moreover so made that I was not able to behold them. And whereas I before esteemed any thing for handsom, here all things so much surpassed the rest, as the Stars in Heaven are elevated. In the mean time the Virgin stept in, and so each of the virgins taking one of us by the hand, with most profound Re-

verence

verence prefented us to the *King*: Whereupon the Virgin began thus to fpeak. *That to honour your Royal Ma-jefties, (moſt gratious King and Queen) theſe Lords here prefent have adventured hither with peril of Body and Life ; your Majefties have reafon to rejoyce, efpecially fince the greateſt part are qualified for the inlarging of your Majeſties Eſtates and Em-pire, as you will find the fame by a moſt gratious and particular examination of each of them. Herewith I was defirous thus to have them in Humility prefented to your Majefties, with moſt humble fuit to dif-charge me of this my Commiſſion, and moſt gratiouſly to take fufficient information from each of them, concerning both my Actions and Omiſſions.* Hereupon fhe laid down her Branch upon the ground. Now it would have been very fitting for one of us to have put in and fpoken fomewhat on this occafion, but feeing we were all troubled with the *falling of* the *Uvula*, at length the old *Atlas* ſtept forward and fpoke on the *King's* behalf; *Their Royal Majefties do moſt gratiouſly re-joyce at your arrival, and will that their Royal Grace be aſſured to all, and every Man : And with thy Adminiſtration, gen-*

the

tle *Virgin*, they are most graciously satisfied, & accordingly a Royal Reward shall therefore be provided for thee; yet it is still their intention, that thou shalt this day also continue with them, in as much as they have no reason to mistrust thee. Hereupon the Virgin humbly took up the Branch again. And so we for this first time were to step aside with our Virgin. This room

Descriptio Laboratorij. was square on the front, five times broader than it was long; but towards the West it had a great Arch like a Porch, wherein stood in circle three

Subsellia. glorious Royal *Thrones*, yet the middlemost was somewhat higher than the rest. Now in each Throne sate two persons,

1. Rex senex Conjux Juven. in the first sate a very antient *King* with a gray Beard, yet his Consort was extraordinary fair and young. In the

3. Rex et conjux senes third Throne sate a black *King* of middle Age, and by him a dainty old Matron, not Crowned, but covered with a Vail. But in the middle sate the two

2. Juvenes. young *Persons*, who tho' they had likewise Wreaths of Laurel upon their Heads, yet over them hung a large and costly *Crown*. Now albeit they were not at this time so fair as I had before imagined to my self, yet so it was to be.

Behind

Behind them on a round Form 'fat for Scamna.
the moſt part *antient* Men, yet none of Aſſeſſores.
them (at which I wondered) had any,
Sword, or other Weapon about him; [Qualeſ-
Neither ſaw I any other Life-guard, nam;] nu
but certain Virgins which were with us illæ virtu-
the day before, who ſate on the ſides of tum?
the Arch. Here can I not paſs in ſilence
how the little *Cupid* flew to and again Cupido.
there, but for the moſt part he hovered and played the wanton about the
great *Crown*; ſometimes he ſeated himfelf in between the two Lovers, ſomewhat ſmiling upon them with his Bow.
Nay, ſometimes he made as if he would
ſhoot one of us; In brief, this *Knave*
was ſo full of his waggery, that he
would not ſpair even the *little Birds,*
which in multitudes flew up and down Aves.
the Room, but tormented them all he
could. The Virgins alſo had their pa- Virgines.
ſtimes with him, but whenſoever they
could catch him, it was not ſo eaſie a
matter for him to *get from* them again.
Thus this little *Knave* made all the
ſport and mirth. Before the *Queen* Supellex i..
ſtood a ſmall, but unexpreſſibly curious Aulâ
Altar: wherin lay a *Book* covered with Altare.
black *Velvet,* only a little over-layed 1. Book.

with *Gold* ; by this ſtood a ſmall Ta-

2. Taper.
per in an *Ivory Candleſtick*, now although it were very *ſmall*, yet it burnt
continually, and ſtood in that manner,
that had not *Cupid*, in ſport, now and
then puffed upon it, we could not have

3. Sphære.
conceived it to be Fire. By this ſtood
a Sphere or Celeſtial Globe, which of

4. Watch.
its ſelf turned clearly about. Next
this, a ſmall ſtriking-Watch, by that

5. little
Fountain.
a little Chriſtal Pipe or *Syphon-Fountain*,
out of which perpetually ran a clear
blood-red Liquor ; and laſt of all a Scull,

6. Scull.

Serpent.
or *Death's-Head* ; in this was a *white
Serpent*, which was of ſuch a length, that
though ſhe crept circle-wiſe about the
reſt of it, yet her Taile ſtill remained in
one of the Eye-holes, until her Head
again entered at the other, ſo ſhe never ſtirred from her Scull, unleſs it
happened that *Cupid* twitched a little
at her, for then ſhe ſlipt in ſo ſuddenly,
that we all could not chooſe but marvel
at it : Together with this *Altar*, there
were up and down the Room wonder-

Imagines.
ful Images, which moved themſelves,
as if they had been alive, and had ſo
ſtrange a contrivance, that it would
be impoſſible for me to relate it all :
like-

likewife as we were paffing out, there began fuch a marvellous kind of vocal Mufick, that I could not certainly tell, *Mufica* whether it were performed by the Virgins who yet ftayed behind, or by the Images themfelves. Now we being for this time fatisfied, went thence with *Difceditur ex laboratorio.* our Virgins, who, the Mufitians being already prefent, led us down the winding Stairs again, but the Door was diligently locked and bolted. As foon as vve were come again into the Hall; one of the Virgins began: *I wonder, Sifter, that you durft adventure your felf amongft fo many Perfons: My Sifter,* replyed our Prefident, *I am fearful of none* *Virgines jocantur de fomnio Autoris.* *fo much as of this Man,* pointing at me; This fpeech went to the Heart of me: For I well underftood that fhe mocked at my *Age,* and indeed I was the oldeft of them all. Yet fhe comforted me again with promife, That in cafe I behaved my felf vvell towards her, fhe vvould eafily rid me of this burden. Mean time a Collation was again *Convivium cum Virginibus.* brought in, and every one's Virgin feated by him, vvho vvell knevv how to fhorten the time with handfom difcourfes: But what their difcourfes

and

Sermones
Convivales.
and sports vvere I dare not blab out of
School. But moſt of the queſtions were
about the Arts, whereby I could lightly gather that both young and old were
converſant in the Sciences. But ſtill it
run in my thoughts hovv I might become young again, whereupon I vvas

Autor
Mæſtus ob
Senium.
ſomevvhat the ſadder ; This the Virgin perceived, and therefore began, *I
dare lay any thing, if I lye with him to
night, he ſhall be pleaſanter in the morning.* Hereupon they began to laugh,
and albeit I bluſhed all over, yet I vvas
fain to laugh too at my ovvn ill-luck.

Jocoſum ſo-
larium
accipit a
Virgine.
Novv there vvas one there that had a
mind to return my diſgrace again upon
the Virgin ; vvhereupon he ſaid, *I
hope not only we, but the Virgins too themſelves will bear witneſs in behalf of our*

Socio.
*Brother, that our Lady Preſident hath pro-
miſed her ſelf to be his Bed-fellow to Night :
I ſhould be well content with it,* replyed the
Virgin, *if I had not reaſon to be afraid of
theſe my Siſters, there would be no hold with
them ſhould I chuſe the beſt and handſomeſt*

Virg. lucif.
for my ſelf, againſt their will. My Siſter
preſently began another, *We find hereby that thy high Office makes thee not proud;
wherefore if by thy permiſſion we might by*
                                                     lot

lot part the Lords here present, amongst us,
for Bed-fellows, thou shouldst with our good-
will have such a Prerogative: We let
this pass thus for a Jeaſt, and began a-
gain to difcourfe together. But our
Virgin could not leave tormenting us,
and therefore began again, *My Lords,*
how if we ſhould permit Fourtune to decide
which of us muſt lie together to Night?
Well, faid I, if it may be no other-
vvife, vve cannot refuſe fuch a proffer.
Novv becauſe it vvas concluded to make
this tryal after Meat, vve reſolved to
fit no longer at Table, ſo we aroſe, and
each one vvalked up and dovvn vvith
his Virgin. *Nay,* faid the Virgin, *It*
ſhall not be ſo yet, but let us fee how For-
tune will couple us ; upon vvhich vve
vvere feparated afunder : But novv firſt
aroſe a difpute hovv the bufinefs ſhould
be carried, but this was only a pre-
meditated device, for the Virgin inftantly
made the propofal that we ſhould mix
our felves together in a Ring, and that
ſhe beginning to count from her felf,
the *feventh,* was to be content with the
following *feventh,* whether it were a
Virgin, or man ; for our parts we
were not aware of any craft, and
therefore

Ludicra
electio urā-
dormientiu.

therefore permitted it so to be ; but
when we thought we had very well
mingled our selves, the Virgins never-
thelefs were so subtil, that each one
knew her station before-hand : The
Virgin began to reckon, the seventh
next her was again a Virgin, the third
seventh a Virgin likewise, and this hapned so long till (to our amazement) all
the *Virgins* came forth, and *none of* us
was hit; Thus we poor pittiful
Wretches remained standing alone, and
were moreover forced to suffer our
selves to be *jeared* too, and confefs we
were very handfomly couzened. In
short, who ever had seen us in our order, might sooner have expected the
Skye to fall, then that it should never
have come to our turn. Herewith our
sport was at an end, and we were fain
to satisfie our selves with the Virgins
Waggery. In the interm, the little
wanton *Cupid* came alfo in unto us ;
But becaufe he presented himfelf on be-
A Health half of their Royal Majesties, and delivered us a Health (as from them) out
of a golden Cup, and was to call our
Virgins to the King, withal declaring
he could at this time tarry no longer
with

with them, we could not sufficiently
sport our selves with him : So with a
due return of our most humble thanks
we let him flye forth again.   Now because (in the interm) the mirth began
to fall into my Consort's Feet, and the
Virgins were nothing sorry to see it, *A merry dance*
they quickly lead up a civil Dance,
whom I rather beheld with pleasure,
then assisted.   For my Mercurialists
were so ready with their Postures,
as if they had been long of the Trade.
After some few Dances, our president *Hospites invitantur a virgine Lucif. ad comædiam*
came in again, and told us how the
Artists and Students had offered themselves to their Royal Majesties, for their
Honour and Pleasure, before their de-
parture to act a Merry Comedy ; and if
we thought good to be present at it,
and to waite upon their Royal Majesties
to the House of the *Sun*, it would be
acceptable to them, and they would
most gratiously acknowledge it : Hereupon in the first place we returned our
most humble thanks for the Honour
vouchsafed us, not only so, but moreover most submissively tendered our
small service, which the Virgin related
again, and presently brought word to
attend

attend their Royal Majesties (in our order) in the Gallery, whither we were
soon led, and staid not long there;
Processus
Regis ad
Spectandam
Comædiam
for the Royal Procession was just ready,
yet without any Musick at all. The
unknown Queen, who was Yesterday
with us, went foremost, with a small and
costly Coronet, apparrelled in *white*
Sattin, she carried nothing but a small
Crucifix which was made of a Pearl,
and this very day wrought between the
young King and his Bride. After her
went the six fore-mentioned Virgins in
two ranks, who carried the King's
Jewels belonging to the little Altar:
next to these came the three Kings.
The Bridegroom was in the midst of
them in a plain dress, only in *black*
Sattin, after the Italian Mode. He had
on a small round black Hat, with a little
black pointed Feather, which he courteously put off to us, thereby to signifie his favour towards us. To him we
bowed our selves, as also to the first, as
we had been before instructed. After the
Kings came the three Queens, two
whereof were richly habited, only she
in the middle went likewise all in *bla.k*,
and Cupid held up her Train; after
this

this Intimation was given to us to follow, and after us the Virgins, till at
last old *Atlas* brought up the rear. In
such Procession, through many stately
Walks, we at length came to the House
of the *Sun*, there next to the King and
Queen, upon a richly furnished Scaffold, Statio
to behold the fore-ordained Comedy : Spectato-
We indeed, though Separated, stood rum.
on the right Hand of the Kings, but
the Virgins on the left, except those, to
whom the Royal Ensignes were committed. To them was allotted a peculiar
standing at top of all. But the rest of
the attendants were fain to stand below
between the columns, and therewith to
be content. Now because there are ma-
ny remarkable Passages in this Comedy, a Præcipuæ
I will not omit in brief to run it over. agebantur,
First of all came forth a very *ancient* Actus. I.
King, with some Servants ; before
whose *Throne* was brought a little *Chest*,
with mention that it was found upon
the Water. Now it being opened, there
appeared in it a lovely *Babe*, together
with certain Jewels, and a small Letter
of Parchment sealed, and superscribed
to the King. Which the King therefore presently opened, and having read
it

L it

it, wept; and then declared to his Servants how injuriously the King of the 𝕸𝖔𝖔𝖗𝖊𝖘 had deprived his Aunt of her Country, and had exftinguifhed all the Royal Seed even to this Infant, with the Daughter of which Country he had now purpofed to have matched his Son. Hereupon he Swore to maintain perpetual enmity with the *Moore*, and his Allies, and to revenge this upon him; and therewith commanded that the Child fhould be tenderly nurfed, and to make preparation againft the *Moore*. Now this provifion and the difcipline of the young Lady (who after fhe was a little grown up was committed to an ancient Tutor) continued all the firft *Act*; with many very fine and laudable fports befides.

Interludi-um. In the interlude a *Lyon and* Griffon were fet at one another, to fight, and the *Lyon* got the victory; which was alfo a pretty fight.

Actus 2. In the fecond *Act*, the *Moore*, a very black treacherous Fellow, came forth alfo; who having with vexation underftood that his Murder was difcovered, and that too a little Lady was craftily ftollen from him; began thereupon to confult how by ftratagem I might

might be able to encounter so powerful
an adversary, whereof he was at length
advised by certain *Fugitives* who by reason of Famine fled to him : So the
young Lady contrary to all mens expectation, fell again into his Hands :
Whom, had he not been wonderfully
deceived by his own Servants, he had
like to have caused to be slain. Thus
this *Act* too was concluded with a mer-
velous triumph of the *Moore*.

 In the third *Act* a great *Army* on the Actus 3.
King's party was raised against the *Moore*,
and put under the conduct of an antient valiant Knight, who fell into the
Moores Country, till at length he forceably rescued the young *Lady* out of
the Tower, and Apparrelled her a new.
After this in a *trice* they erected a glorious Scaffold, and placed their young
Lady upon it : presently came *twelve*
Royal Embassadors, amongst whom the
fore-mentioned Knight made a Speech,
alledging that the King his most gracious
Lord had not only heretofore delivered
her from death, and even hitherto caused her to be royally brought up (though
she had not behaved her self altogether
as became her) But moreover his Royal
H Majesty

Majesty had, before others, elected
her, to be a Spouse for the young *Lord*
his Son; and most gratiously desired
that the said espousals might be really
executed in case they would be sworn
to his Majesty upon the following Arti-
cles. Hereupon out of a Patent he caused certain glorious conditions to be
read, which if it were not too long,
were well worthy to be here recounted.
In brief, the young Lady took an Oath
inviolably to observe the same; return-
ing thanks withal in most seemly sort
for this so high a Grace. Whereupon
they began to sing to the Praise of God,
of the King, and the young Lady; and
so for this time departed.

Interludium

For sport, in the mean while, the
four Beasts of *Daniel*, as he saw them
in the Vision, and hath at large descri-
bed them, were brought in, all which
had its certain *signification*.

Actus 4.

In the fourth *Act* the young Lady was
again *restored* to her lost Kingdom, and
Crowned, and for a space, in this array,
conducted about the place with extraordinary joy: after this many & various
Embassadors presented themselves, not
only to wish her prosperity, but also

to

to behold her Glory. Yet it was not long that she preserved her Integrity, but soon began again to look wantonly about her, and to wink at the Embassadors and Lords; wherein she truly acted her part to the Life.

These her manners were soon known to the *Moore*, who would by no means neglect such an opportunity, and because her Steward had not sufficient regard to her, she was easily blinded with great promises, so that she had no good confidence in her King, but privily submitted her self to the intire disposal of the *Moore*. Hereupon the *Moore* made haste, and having (by her consent) gotten her into his Hands, he gave her good words so long till all her Kingdom had subjected it self to him: After which in the third Scene of this *Act*, he caused her to be led forth, and first to be stript stark naked, and then upon a scurvy wooden Scaffold to be bound to a Post, and well scourged, and at last sentenced to *Death*. This was so woful a Spectacle, that it made the Eyes of many to run over. Hereupon thus *naked* as she was, she was cast into Prison, there to expect her Death, which was

to

to be procured by *Poyſon*, which yet
killed her not, but made her Leprous
all over : Thus this *Act* was for the
Interludium. moſt part lamentable.

Between, they brought forth 𝕹𝖊𝖇𝖚-
𝖈𝖍𝖆𝖉𝖓𝖊𝖟𝖟𝖆𝖗'𝖘 Image, which was adorn'd
with all manner of Arms, on the Head,
Breaſt, Belly, Legs and Feet, and the
like ; of which too more ſhall be ſpoken
in the future explication.

Actus. 5. In the fifth *Act* the young King was
acquainted with all that had paſſed between the *Moore* and his future Spouſe,
who firſt interceeded with his Father
for her, intreating that ſhe might not
be left in that condition ; which his
Father having agreed to, Embaſſadors
were diſpatched to comfort her in her
Sickneſs and Captivity, but yet, withal to give her notice of her inconſidera-
tedneſs. But ſhe would not yet receive
them, but conſented to be the *Moore's*
Concubine, which was alſo done, and the
young King was acquainted with it.

Interludium. After this comes a band of Fools, each
of which brought with him a Cudgel,
where with in a trice they made a great
Globe of the World, and as ſoon undid
it again. It was a fine ſportive Phantſie.

In

In the sixth *Act* the young King re- solved to bid battle to the *Moore*, which also was done. And albeit the *Moore* was discomfitted, yet all held the young King too for dead. At length he came to himself again, released his Spouse, and committed her to his Steward and Chaplain.

The first whereof tormented her mightily, at last the leaf turned over, and the Priest was so insolently wicked, that he would needs be above all, until the same was reported to the young King, who hastily dispatched one who broke the Neck of the Priest's mightiness, and adorned the Bride in some measure for the Nuptials.

After the *Act* a vast artificial *Elephant* was brought forth. He carried a great Tower with Musitians: which was also well-pleasing to all.

In the last *Act* the Bride-groom appeared in such pomp as is not well to be believed, and I was amazed how it was brought to pass: The Bride met him in the like Solemnity. Whereupon all the People cried out *VIVAT* *SPONSUS, VIVAT SPONSA.* So that by this Comedy they did with all congratulate our King and Queen in the

most

moſt ſtately manner : Which (as I well
obſerved) pleaſed them moſt extraordinary well.

At length they made ſome paſces
about the ſtage in ſuch Proceſſion, till at
laſt they altogether began thus to
Sing.

I

Cantilena.
*This time full of love
Does our joy much improve
Because of the King's Nuptial ;
And therefore let's Sing
That from all parts 't may ring,
Bleß be he that granted us all.*

II

*The Bride moſt exquiſitely faire :
Whom we attended with long care
To him in troth's now plighted :
We fully have at length obtain'd,
The ſame for which we did contend :
He's happy, that's fore-ſighted.*

III

*Now the Parents Kind and good
By intreaties are ſubdu'd :
Long enough in hold was ſhe mew'd ;
In honour increaſe,
Till* **Thouſands** *ariſe.
And ſpring from your own proper Blood.*

Epilogus. After this thanks were returned, and
the

the Comedy was finiſhed with joy, and
the particular good liking of the Royal Perſons wherefore (the Evening alſo
being already hard by) they departed
together in their fore-mentioned order:
But we were to attend the Royal Perſons up the winding Stairs into the
forementioned Hall, where the Tables
were already richly furniſhed, and this
was the firſt time that we were invited
to the Kings table. The little Altar was
placed in the midſt of the Hall, and the
ſix fore-named Royal Enſignes were
laid on it. At this time the young King
behaved himſelf very gratiouſly towards
us; but yet he could not be heartily
Merry ; But howbeit he now and then
diſcourſed a little with us, yet he often
ſighed, at which the little Cupid only
mocked, and playd his waggiſh tricks.
The old King and Queen were very ſe-
rious, only the *Wife* of one of the ancient Kings was gay enough; the cauſe
whereof I yet underſtood not. During this, the Royal Perſons took up the
firſt Table, at the ſecond we only Sate.
At the third, ſome of the principal
Virgins placed themſelves : The reſt of
the Virgins, and Men, were all fain to
wait

Marginal notes:
Hoſpites in-
vitantur ad
cænam Re-
gis et Re-
ginæ.

Rex Addi-
leſc.

Reges
Adulti.

Ordo dis-
cumcbati-
um.

wait. This was performed with such state and solemn stilness, that I am afraid to make many words of it. Here I cannot leave untouched how that all the Royal Persons, before Meat, attired themselves in *Snow*-white glittering Garments, and so sate down to Table. Over the Table hung the fore-mentioned great Golden Crown, the pretious Stones whereof, without any other Light, would have sufficiently illuminated the Hall. However all the Lights were kindled at the *small Taper* upon the Altar; what the reason was I did not certainly know. But this I took very good notice of, that the young King frequently sent Meat to the white *Serpent* upon the little Altar, which caused me to muse. Almost all the Prattle at this Banquet was made by little Cupid, who could not leave us (and me indeed especially) untormented. He was perpetually producing some *Strange* matter. However, there was no considerable Mirth, all went silently on; from whence I, by my self, could imagin some great imminent Peril. For there was no Musick at all heard; but if we were demanded any thing,

we

Ornatus vestium.

Corona Super Mensam.

Cupido was the Merriest

we were fain to give short round an- Sermones breves
wers, and so let it rest. In short, all
things had so strange a face, that the
sweat began to trickle down all over my
body ; and I am apt to believe that the
stout-heartedst Man alive would then
have lost his courage. Supper being
now almost ended, the young King
commanded the Book to be reached him
from the little Altar. This he opened, Oratio Regis Adolefcentis.
and caused it once again by an old Man
to be propounded to us, whether we
resolved to abide with him in *Prosperity*
and Adversity ; which we having with
trembling consented to, he further
caused us sadly to be demanded, whether we would give him our Hands on
it, which, when we could find no evasi-
on, was fain so to be. Hereupon one
after another arose, and with his own
Hand writ himself down in this Book.
When this also was performed, the
little *Chrystal Fountain*, together with a
very small Chrystal Glass was brought A Health.
near, out of which all the Royal Persons
one after *another Drank*, afterwards it
was reached to us too, and so forward
to all Persons, and this was called, *the*
Draught of Silence. Hereupon all the Haustus de silentio.
                                    Royal

Royal Perſons preſent(
Hands, declaring that in ca
now ſtick to them, we ſh(
never more hereafter ſee·t

Fidejubetur
Virg. Lucif· verily made our Eyes run
our preſident engaged her
miſed very largely on our
gave them Satisfaction.
little Bell was tolled, at w
Royal Perſons waxed ſo r
that we were ready utter
They quickly put off the
ments again, and put on i(
ones; The whole Hall. l

Mors Re- hung about with black Vel(
gulorum.
was covered with black
which alſo the Cieling ab
being before Prepared.)
ſpread. After that the
alſo removed away, and a
themſelves round about
Form; and we alſo had |
habits ; in comes our Pre
who was before gone out,
with her ſix black Taffata
which ſhe bound the *ſix* ,
Eyes. Now when they co(
ſee, there were immediatel
by the Servants ſix covere(

et down in the Hall, alfo a low black
feat placed in the midft. Finally, there
ftept in a very cole-black tall Man, who
bare in his hand a fharp Ax: Now af- De collatio
ter that the old King had been firft Regum.
brought to the Seat, his *Head* was inftantly whipt off, and wrapped up in a
black Cloth, but the *Blood* was received
into a great *golden Goblet*, and placed
with him in the Coffin that ft ood by,
which being covered, vvas fet afide.
Thus it went with the reft alfo, fo
that I thought it would at length have
come to me too, but it did not; For as
foon as the fix *Royal Perfons* were Beheaded, the black Man vvent out again;
after vvhom another follovved, vvho
Beheaded *him* too juft before the Door,
and brought back his Head together Carnificis.
vvith the Ax, vvhich vvere laid in a
little Cheft. This indeed to me feemed a bloody Wedding , but becaufe I
could not tell vvhat vvould yet be the
event, I vvas fain for that time to cap-
tivate my underftanding until I vvere
further refolved. For the Virgin too, Hofpites
feeing that fome of us vvere faint-*hearted* Mærent.
and vvept, bid us be content. For,
faid fhe to us, *The Life of thefe ftandeth* Solatium
now

now in your hands, and in cast you follow me, this Death shall make many alive. Herewith she intimated we should go sleep, & trouble our selves no further on our part, for they should be sure to have their due right; And so she bad us all good night, saying, *That she must watch the dead Corps this night*: We did so, and were each of us conducted by our Pages into our Lodgings. My Page talked with me of sundry and various matters (which I still very well remember) and gave me cause enough to admire at his understanding: But his intention was to lull me asleep, which at last I well observed, whereupon I made as though I was fast asleep, but no sleep came into my Eyes, and I could not put the Beheaded out of my mind. Now my Lodging was directly over against the great *Lake*, so that I could well look upon it, the Windows being nigh the Bed. About midnight, as soon as it had struck twelve, on a sudden I espied on the *Lake* a great *Fire*, wherefore out of fear I quickly opened the Window to see what would become of it; Then from far I saw seven *Ships* making forward, which were all stuck full

Cura Noctuna mortuorum.

Hospites eunt cubitum.

Cubiculum

Visio nocturna.

full

full of Lights, Above on the top of
each of them hovered a *Flame*, that paffed to and fro, and fometimes defcended quite down, fo that I could lightly
judge that it muft needs be the *Spirit* of
the Beheaded. Now thefe Ships gently approached to Land, and each of them
had no more than one Mariner. As foon
as they were now gotten to Shore, I
prefently efpied our Virgin with a
Torch going towards the Ships, after
whom the fix covered Coffins, together
with the little Cheft, were carried ; and
each of them privily laid in a Ship.
Wherefore I awaked my Page too, who   Cadavera
hugely thanked me, for having run much   aveh r
up and down all the day, he might quite translacura
have over-flept this, tho' he well knew
it. Now as foon as the Coffins were
laid in the Ships, all the Lights *were* ex-
tinguifhed, and the fix *Flames* paffed
back together over the *Lake*, fo that
there was no more but one Light in each
Ship for a Watch. There were alfo
fome hundreds of Watch-men who had
encamped themfelves on the Shore, and
fent the Virgin back again into the Caftle, who carefully bolted all up again ;

fo

fo that I could well judge that there was nothing more to be done this night, but that we muft expect the day ; fo we again betook our felves to reft. And I only of all my Company had a Chamber towards the Lake, and faw this, fo *Autor folus, hæc vidit.* that now I was alfo extream weary, and fo fell afleep in my manifold Speculations.

The fifth Day.

Obambulatio antelucana. THe night was over, and the dear wifhed for day broken, when haftily I got me out of the Bed, more defirous to learn what might yet infue, than that I had fufficiently flept; Now after that I had put on my Cloaths, and according to my cuftom was gone down the Stairs, it was ftill too early, and I found no body elfe in the Hall, wherefore I intreated my Page to lead me a little about in the Caftle, and fhew me fomewhat that was rare, who was now (as always) willing, and prefently lead me down certain fteps under ground, to a great Iron Door, on which the following Words in great Copper Letters, were fixed. This

[decorative cipher script]

VENVS

[decorative cipher script]

[decorative cipher script]

[decorative cipher script]

This I thus copied, and set down in
my Table-Book. Now after this Door
was opened, the Page led me by the
hand through a very dark Paſſage, till
we came again to a very little Door,
that was now only put too, For (as
the Page informed me) it was firſt
opened but yeſterday when the Coffins
were taken out, and had not been ſince
ſhut. Now as ſoon as we ſtepped in, I
eſpied the moſt pretious thing that Nature ever created : For this Vault had
no other light but from certain huge
great *Carbuncles* ; And this (as I was informed) was the *King's Treaſury.* But
the moſt glorious and principal thing,
that I here ſaw, was a *Sepulcher* (which
ſtood in the midſle) ſo rich that I wondred it was no better guarded ; whereunto

[margin note:] Thalamus Veneris ſe-
pulcræ.

[margin note:] Theſaurus Regis.

unto the Page anſwered me, *That I had good reaſon to be thankful to my Planet, by whoſe influence it was, that I had now ſeen certain pieces which no humane Eye elſe (except the King's Family) had ever had a view of.* This Sepulcher was *triangular,* and had in the middle of it a Kettle of poliſhed Copper, the reſt was of pure Gold and pretious Stones ; In the Kettle ſtood an Angel, who held in his Arms an unknown Tree, from which it continually dropped into the Kettle ; and as oft as the Fruit fell into the Kettle, it turned into *Water* too, and ran out from thence into three ſmall Golden Kettles ſtanding by. This little Altar was ſupported by theſe three Animals, an *Eagle,* an *Ox* and a Lyon, which ſtood on an exceeding coſtly Baſe. I asked my Page what this might ſignifie: *Here,* ſaid he, *lies Buried* Lady Venus, *that Beauty which hath undone many a great Man, both in Fourtune, Honour, Bleſſing and Proſperity.* After which he ſhewed me a Copper Door on the Pavement. *Here* (ſaid he) *if you pleaſe, we may go further down;*I ſtill follow you (replyed I) ſo I went down the ſteps, where it was exceeding dark, but the Page immediately

Deſcriptio Sepulchri.

Aliud Triclinium.

diately opened a little Cheſt, wherein
ſtood a ſmall *ever-burning Taper*, at
which he kindled one of the many
Torches which lay by. I was mightily terrified, and ſeriouſly asked how he
durſt do this? He gave me for anſwer, *As long as the Royal Perſons are
ſtill at reſt, I have nothing to fear.* Herewith I eſpied a rich Bed ready made,
hung about with curious Curtains, one
of which he drew, where I ſaw the
Lady *Venus ſtark-naked* (for he heaved up
the Coverlets too) lying there in ſuch
Beauty, and a faſhion ſo ſurprizing, that
I was almoſt beſides my ſelf, neither
do I yet know whether it was a piece
thus Carved, or an humane Corps
that lay dead there; For ſhe was altogether immoveable, and yet I durſt not
touch her. So ſhe was again covered,
and the Curtain drawn before her,
yet ſhe was ſtill (as it were) in my Eye.
But I ſoon eſpyed behind the Bed a Tablet, on which it was thus written.

*Deſcriptio
corporis
Veneris dor-
micatis.*

7

I asked my Page concerning this
Writing, but he laughed, with promise that I should know it too. So he
putting out the Torch, we again afcend-
ed. Then I better viewed all the little Doors, and firft found, that on e-
very corner there burned a fmall Taper
of *Pyrites*, of which I had before taken no notice; for the Fire was fo clear,
that it looked much liker a Stone than
a Taper. From this heat the Tree was
forced continually to *melt*, yet it ftill
produced new Fruit. *Now behold* (faid
the Page) *what I heard revealed to the
King by* Atlas, *When the Tree* (faid he)
fhall be quite melted down, Then fhall Lady
Venus *awake, and be the Mother of a* King.
Whilft

Arbor: ca-
lor ex faci-
bus.

Whilſt he was thus ſpeaking, in flew
the little Cupid, who at firſt was ſomewhat abaſhed at our preſence, but ſee-
ing us both look more like the Dead *Mulča ſe-*
then the Living, he could not at length *ča hujus*
refrain from Laughing, *Demanded what* *obambulati-*
Spirit had brought me thither, whom I with *bnis.*
trembling anſwered, that I had loſt my
way in the Caſtle, and was by chance
come hither, and that the Page likewiſe had been looking up and down for
me, and at laſt lited upon me here, I
hoped he would not take it amiſs. *Nay,*
then 'tis well enough yet, ſaid Cupid, *my*
old buſie Granſir, but you might lightly have
ſerved me a ſcurvy trick, had you been a-
ware of this Door. *Now I muſt look bet-*
ter to it, and ſo he put a ſtrong Lock on
the Copper Door, where we before deſcended. I thanked God that he lited
upon us no ſooner, my Page too was
the more jocond, becauſe I had ſo well
helped him at this pinch. *Yet can I*
not (ſaid Cupid) *let it paſs unrevenged,*
that yon were ſo near ſtumbling upon my dear
Mother; with that he put the point of
his Dart into one of the little Tapers,
and heating it a little, pricked me with
it on the hand, which at that time I lit-

I 2   tle

tle regarded, but was glad that it went
ſo well with us, and that we came off
without further danger. Mean time my
Companions were gotten out of Bed
too, and were again returned into the
Hall. To whom I alſo joyned my ſelf,
making as if I were then firſt riſen.
After Cupid had carefully made all faſt
again, he came likewiſe to us, and
would needs have me ſhew him my
hand, where he ſtill found a little drop

of blood, at which he heartily laughed,
and bad the reſt have a care of me, I
would ſhortly end my days. We all
wondred how Cupid could be ſo merry,

and have no ſence at all of the yeſterday's ſad paſſages. But he was no whit
troubled. Now our Preſident had in

the mean time made her ſelf ready for
the Journey, coming in all in *black Velvet*, yet ſhe ſtill bare her branch of Laurel, her Virgins too had their Branches.
Now all things being in readineſs, the
Virgin bid us firſt drink ſomevvhat, and
then preſently prepare for the proceſſion ; wherefore we made no long tarrying, but follovved her out of the
Hall into the Court. In the Court ſtood
ſix Coffins, and my Companions thought
no other but that the ſix Royal Perſons
lay

lay in them, but I well obſerved the device: Yet I knew not what was to be
done with theſe other. By each Coffin
were eight *muffled* Men. Now as ſoon
as the Muſick went (it was ſo mournful
& doleſome a tune, that I was aſtoniſhed
at it) they took up the Coffins, and we
(as we were ordered) were fain to go
after them into the formentioned Garden, in the midſt of which was erected
a wooden Edifice, having round about
the Roof a glorious Crown, and ſtanding *upon ſeven* Columns; within it were
formed ſix Sepulchers, and by each of
them a ſtone, but in the middle it had a
round hollow riſing ſtone: In theſe Graves
the Coffins were quietly and with many
Cerimonies layed: The ſtones were ſho-
ved over them, and they ſhut faſt. But
the little Cheſt was to lie in the middle.
Herewith were my Companions deceived, for they imagined no other but
that the Dead Corps were there. Upon
the top of all there was a great Flag, having a *Phenix* painted on it, perhaps
therewith the more to delude us. Here
I had great occaſion to thank God that I
had ſeen more than the reſt. Now af- Hoſpites vo-
ter the Funerals were done, the Virgin, cantur ad labores provi-
I 3 having ta Regum.

having placed her felf upon the middle-
moft Stone, made a fhort Oration, *That*
we fhould be conftant to our ingagements,
and not repine at the pains we were hereafter
to undergo, but be helpful in reftoring the
prefent buried Royal Perfons *to* Life *again,*
and therefore without delay to rife up with
her, to make a Journey to the Tower of
Olympus, *to fetch from thence Medicines*
ufeful and neceffary for this purpofe. This
we foon agreed to, and followed her
through another little door quite to the
Shore. There the feven fore-mentioned *Ships* ftood all empty; on which all
the Virgins ftuck up their *Laurel*
Branches, and after they had diftributed
us in the fix Ships, they caufed us in
Gods name ; thus to begin our Voyage,
and looked upon us as long as they could
have us in fight, after which they with
all the Watch-men, returned into the
Caftle. Our Ships had each of them a
peculiar device. Five of them indeed
had the five *regular Bodies,* each a feveral one, but mine in which the Virgin
too fate, carried a Globe. Thus we
failed on in a fingular order, and each
had only two Mariners. Foremoft went
the Ship *a,* in which, as I conceive the

Moor

Moſt lay, in this were *twelve Muſitians,*
who played excellent well, its device
was a Pyramid. Next followed three
a breaſt, *b, c,* and *d,* in vvhich vve were
diſpoſed, I ſate in *c.* In the midſt behind theſe came the two faireſt and
ſtatelieſt Ships, *e* and *f,* ſtuck about
with many Branches of Laurel, having
no Paſſengers in them ; their Flags were
the *Sun* and *Moon.* But in the rear only one Ship *g,* in this vvere *Forty Vir-*
gins. Novv being thus paſſed over this
Lake, we firſt came through a narrovv
Arm, into the right Sea, where all the
Syrens, Nymphs, and Sea-Goddeſſes had
attended us ; wherefore they immediately diſpatched a Sea-Nymph to us to
deliver their Preſent and Offering of
Honour to the Wedding. It was a
coſtly, great, ſet, round, and Orient
Pearl; the like to vvhich hath not at a-
ny time been ſeen, either in ours, or
yet in the nevv World. Novv the Virgin having friendly received it, the
Nymph further intreated that audience
might be given to their Divertiſements,
and to make a little ſtand, vvhich the
Virgin vvas content to do, and commanded the tvvo great Ships to ſtand

a

b c d

e f

g

40 Virgines
comites.

Excipiuntur
a Nymphis.

into

c
b// ⹀d
e‖ ‖f

g\\ //a

into the middle, and
with the reſt to in-
compaſs them in
Pentagon. After
which the Nymphs
fell into a ring a-
bout them, and with a moſt delicate
ſvveet voice began thus to ſing.

I

There's nothing better here below
Than beauteous, noble, Love ;
Whereby we like to God do grow,
And none to grief do move.
Wherefore let's chant it to the King,
That all the Sea thereof may ring.
We queſtion ; Anſwer you.

I I

What was it that at firſt us made ?
'Twas Love.
And what hath Grace a freſh conveigh'd ?
'Tis Love.
Whence was't (pray tell us) we were born ?
Of Love.
How came we then again forlorn ?
Sans Love.

I I I.

Who was it (ſay) that us conceived ?
'Twas Love.

Who

Who Suckled, Nurſed, and Reliev'd?
       'Twas Love.
What is it we to our Parents owe?
       'Tis Love.
Why do they us ſuch kindneſs ſhow?
       Of Love.

IV

Who get's herein the Victory?
       'Tis Love.
Can Love by ſearch obtained be?
       By Love.
How may a Man good works perform?
       Through Love.
Who into one can two transform?
       'Tis Love.

V.

Then let our Song ſound,
Till it's Eccho rebound.
To Loves honour and praiſe,
Which may ever encreaſe
With our noble Princes, the King, & the Queen,
The Soul is departed, their Body's within.

VI

And as long as we live,
God graciouſly give;
That, as great Love and Amity,
They bear each other mightily;
So we likewiſe, by Loves own Flame,
May reconjoyn them once again.

VII.

VII.

Then this annoy
Into great Joy
(If many thousand younglings deign)
Shall change, and ever so remain.

Autori perplacent Nymphæ et cantus. They having with most admirable concent and melody finished this Song, I no more Wondred at *Ulisses* for stopping the Ears of his Companions; for I seemed to my self the most unhappy man alive, that Nature had not made me too so trim a creature. But the *Virgin* soon dispatched them, and commanded to set Sail from thence; wherefore the Nymphs too after they had been presented with a long red *Scarff* for a gratuity; went off, and dispersed themselves in the Sea. I was at this time sensible, that *Cupid* began to work with me too, which yet tended but very little to my Credit, and for as much as my giddiness is likely to be nothing beneficial to the Reader, I am resolved to let it rest as it is. But this was the very wound that in the first Book I received on the head in a Dream: and let every one take warning by me of

The Nimphs are rewarded.

Autori desunt adhuc duo.

loitering

loitering about *Venus's* Bed, for *Cupid*
can by no means brook it. After some
Hours, having in friendly discourses
made a good way, we came within Ken
of the Tower of *Olympus*; wherefore the
Virgin commanded by the discharge of
some Pieces to give the signal of our
approach, which was also done; And
immediately we espyed a great *white*
Flag thrust out, and a small gilded Turris
Pinnace sent forth to meet us. Now Olympi.
as soon as this was come to us, we perceived in it a very ancient man, the
Warden of the Tower; with certain Custos.
Guards cloathed in *white*, of whom we
were Friendly received; and so conducted to the Tower. This Tower
was Situated upon an *Island* exactly
square, which was invironed with a *Wall* Structure,
so firm and thick, that I my self count-
ed two hundred and *sixty* passes over. Dies.
On the other side of the wall was a fine
Meadow with certain little Gardens, in
which grew strange, and to me unknown, Fruits; and then again an
inner Wall round about the Tower.
The Tower of it self was just as if
seven round Towers had been built one
by another, yet the middlemost was
some

somewhat the higher, and within they all entred one into another, and had seven Storys one above another. Being thus come to the Gates of the Tower, we were led a little aside on the Wall, that so, as I well observed, the Coffins might be brought into the Tower without our taking notice; of this the rest knew nothing. This being done, we were conducted into the Tower at the

1.Concloave very bottom, which albeit it were excellently painted, yet we had here littil recreation, for this was nothing but a *Laboratory*, where we were fain to beat and wash Plants, and pretious Stones,

Labores hospitum. and all Sorts of Things, and extract their Juice and Essence, and put up the same in Glasses, and deliver them to be laid up. And truly our Virgin was so busie with us, and so full of her directions, that she knew how to give each of us employment enough, so that in this Island we were fain to be meer *drudges, till* we had atcheived all that was necessary for the restoring of the Beheaded Bodies. Mean time (as I afterwards understood) three Virgins were

Virginum in the first Apartment washing the Corps with all diligence. Now having

at

at *length almoſt* done with this our preparation, nothing more was brought us,
but ſome broath with a little draught of
Wine, whereby I well obſerved, that
we were not here for our pleaſure ; for
when we had finiſhed our days work too,
every one had only a Mattreſs laid on
the Ground for him, wherewith we
were to content our ſelves. For my
part I was not very much troubled with
ſleep, and therefore walked out into
the Garden, and at length came as far
as the Wall ; and becauſe the Heaven
was at that time very clear, I could well
drive away the time in contemplating
the *Stars* ; By chance I came to a great
pair of Stone-Stairs, which led up to
the top of the Wall. And becauſe the
Moon ſhone very bright, I was ſo much
the more confident, and went up, and
looked too a little upon the Sea, which
was now exceeding calm ; and thus having good opportunity to conſider better of Aſtronomy, I found that this preſent Night there would happen ſuch a
conjunction of the Planets, the like to
which was not otherwiſe ſuddenly to be
obſerved. Now having looked a good
while into the Sea, and it being juſt a-
bout

Margin notes:
Cibus
Potus

Lectus.
tenuis.

Autor Spe-
culatur cæ-
lum pro-
ſomno.

bout Midnight, as foon as it had ftruck
Twelve, I beheld from far the *feven*
Flames paffing over Sea hitherward, and
betakeing themfelves to the top of the
Spire of the Tower. This made me
fomewhat affraid ; for as foon as the
Flames had fetled themfelves, the
Winds arofe, and began to make the
Sea very Tempeftuous. The Moon alfo was Covered with cloqds, and my
joy ended with fuch fear, that I had
fcarce time enough to hit upon the Stairs
again, and betake my felf again to the
Tower. Now whether the Flames
tarried any longer, or paffed a-
way again, I cannot fay : For in this
obfcurity I durft no more venture a-
broad : So I laid me down upon my
Mattrefs, and there being befides in the
Laboratory a pleafant and gently purling
Fountain, I fell a Sleep fo much the
fooner. And thus this fifth day too was
concluded with Wonders.

The

The Sixth Day.

NExt morning, after we had awaked one another, we fate together
a while to difcourfe what might yet be
the event of things. For fome were of
opinion that they fhould all be inlivened
again together! Others contradicted
it, becaufe the deceafe of the ancients
was not only to *reftore* life, but increafe
too to the young ones. Some imagined
that they were not put to death, but
that others were beheaded in their ftead.
We having now talked together a pretty while. in comes the Old Man to us,
and firft faluting us, looks about him
to fee if all things were ready, and the
proceffes enough done. We had herein
fo behaved our felves, that he had no
fault to find with our diligence, whereupon he placed all the Glaffes together,
and put them into a cafe. Prefently
come certain youths bringing with them
fome *Ladders*, *Roapes*, and large Wings,
which they laid down before us, and
departed. Then the old Man began
thus.

[marginal notes:]
De fine ortæ dubiæ opiniones.

Cuftos.

pyrotechnia hofpitum laudatur

pueri armiferi

thus. My Dear Sons, one of these three things must each of you this day constantly bear about with him. Now it is free for you either to make a choice of one of them, or to cast lots about it. We replied, we would choose. Nay; said he, let it rather go by lot. Hereupon he made three little Schedules, in one he writ *Ladder*, on the second *Rope*, on the third *Wings*; These he laid in an Hat, and each man must draw, and whatever he happened upon, that was to be his. Those who got the *Ropes*, imagined themselves to be in the best case, but I chanced on a *Ladder*, which hugely afflicted me, for it was twelve-foot long, and pretty weighty, and I must be forced to carry it, whereas the others could handsomly coyle their Ropes about them: and as for the *Wings*, the old Man joyned them so neatly on to the third sort, as if they had grown upon them. Hereupon he turned the Cock, and then the Fountain ran no longer, and we were fain to remove it, from the middle out of the way. After all things were carried off, he taking with him the Casket with the Glasses, took leave, and lock

ed the Door faſt after him, ſo that we imagined no other but that we had been
impriſoned in this Tower.   But it was _{Aſcenſus}
hardly a quarter of an Hour before a _{clave.}
round Hole at the very *top* was uncover-
ed, where we ſaw our Virgin, who called to us, and bad us good Morrow,
deſiring us *to come* up.   They with the
Wings were inſtantly above through
the hole.   Only they with the Ropes
were in evil plight.   For as ſoon as e-
ver'one of us was up, he was commanded to draw up the Ladder to him.   At
laſt each mans Rope was hanged on an _{Reſtis}
Iron Hook, ſo every one was fain to _{difficultas}
climb up by his Rope as well as he could,
which indeed was not compaſſed without Bliſters.   Now as ſoon as we were
all well up, the hole was again covered,
and we were friendly received by the
Virgin.   This Room was the whole
breadth of the Tower it ſelf, having
Six very ſtately *Veſtries* a little raiſed
above the Room, and to be entred by
the aſcent of three Steps.   In theſe _{Deſcriptio}
Veſtries we were diſtributed, there to _{2 Conciav.}
pray for the Life of the King and Queen,
mean while the Virgin went in and
out at the little Door *a*, till we had done.
For as ſoon as our proceſs was abſolved,

K there

there was brought in, and placed in the middle through the little Door, by twelve perſons (which were formerly our Muſitians) a wonderful thing of a *longiſh* ſhape, which my Companions took only to be a Fountain. But I well obſerved that the *Corps's* lay in it, for the inner Cheſt was of an oval Figure, ſo large that ſix Perſons might well lie in it one by another. After which they again went forth, fetched their Inſtruments, and conducted in our Virgin, together with her ſhe-attendants, with a moſt delicate noiſe of Muſick. The Virgin carried a little Caſket, but the reſt only Branches, and ſmall Lamps, and ſome too lighted Torches. The Torches were immediately given into our Hands, and we were to ſtand about the Fountain in this order.

The little Caſket.

Ordo chori.

Firſt ſtood the *Virgin* A with her attendants in a Ring, round about with the Lamps & branches *c*, next ſtood we with our Torches *b*, then the *Muſitians a* in a long rank, laſt

of

of all the reſt of the Virgins *d* in another
long rank too. Now whence the Virgins
came, or whether they dwelt in the
Caſtle, or whether they were brought
in by night, I know not, for all their
Faces were covered with delicate white
Linnen, ſo that I could not know any *virgines* *d*
of them.   Hereupon the Virgin open- *unde.*
ed the Casket, in which there was a *Quid in ar-*
round thing wrapped up in a piece of *cula.*
green double Taffata.   This ſhe laid in
the uppermoſt Kettle, and then covered it with the lid, which was full of
holes, and had beſides a Rim, on which
ſhe poured in ſome of the Water
which we had the day before prepared,
whence the Fountain began immediately to run, and through four ſmall Pipes
to drive into the little Kettle ; beneath
the undermoſt Kettle there were many
ſharp points, on which the Virgins ſtuck
their Lamps, that ſo the heat might
come to the Kettle, and make the Water Seeth.   Now the Water beginning
to Simper, by many little holes at *a*, it
fell in upon the Bodies, and was ſo hot,
that it *diſſolved* them all, and turned them
into Liquor.   But what the aboveſaid
round wrapt up thing was, my Companions knew not, but I underſtood

that it was the Moor's Head, from which the Water conceived so great heat. At *b* round about the great Kettle, there were again many holes, in which

Rami lau-
res.

they stuck their Branches; now whether this was done of necessity, or only for Ceremony, I know not; However these Branches were continually besprinkled by the Fountain, whence it afterwards dropt somewhat of a deeper *Yellow* into the Kettle. This lasted for near two Hours, that the Fountain still constantly ran of it self; but yet the longer, the fainter it was. Mean time the Musitians went their vvay, and vve walked up and down in the Room ; and

Deliciæ in
Conclavi

truly the Room was so made, that we had opportunity enough to pass away our time: There was, for Images, Paintings, Clock-works, Organs, Springing Fountains, and the like, nothing forgotten. Now it was near the time that the Fountain ceased, and would run no longer: upon which the Virgin commanded a round Golden Globe to be brought. But at the bottom of the Fountain there was a Tap, by which she let out all the matter that was dissolved by those hot Drops (whereof certain

tain quarts were then *very Red)* into the Globe. The reft of the Water which remained above in the Kettle, was poured out. And fo this Fountain (which was now become much lighter) was again carried forth. Now whether it was opened abroad, or whether any thing of the Bodies that was further ufeful, yet remained, I dare not certainly fay : But this I know, that the Water that was emptied into the Globe was much *heavier* then *fix*, or yet more of us were well able to bear, albeit for its bulk it fhould have feemed not too heavy for one man. Now this Globe being with much ado gotten out of Doors, we again fate alone. But I perceiving a trampling over head, had an Eye to my Ladder. Hear one might take notice of the ftrange opinions my Companions had concerning this Fountain : For they not imagining but that the Bodies lay in the Garden of the Caftle, knew not what to make of this kind of working, but I thanked God that I awaked in fo opportune a time, and faw that which helped me the better in all the Virgins bufinefs. After one quarter of an hour the cover

Gravitas aquæ.

Autor folus novit veré quæ ageretur.

K 4 above

above was again lifted of, and we commanded to come up, which was done as before vvith Wings, Ladders, and Ropes. And it did not a little vex me, that vvhereas the Virgins could go up another vvay, vve vvere fain to take so much toil; yet I could vvell *[ ] [ ]* there muft be some *special* reafon *[ ]* it, and vve muft leave fomevvhat *[ ] [ ]* he *Old Man* to do too. For even *[ ] [ ]* vvith the Wings had no advantage *[ ]* them but vvhen they vvere to mount through the Hole. Novv being gotten up thither alfo, and the Hole fhut again, I favv the Globe hanging by a ftrong Chain in the middle of the Room. In this Room vvas nothing elfe but meer Windovvs, and ftill betvveen two *Windows* there vvas a Door, vvhich vvas covered vvith nothing but a great polifhed Looking-Glafs ; and thefe Windovvs and Looking-Glaffes were fo optically oppofed one to another, that although the Sun (vvhich novv fhined exceeding bright) beat only upon one Door, yet (after the Windovvs tovvards the Sun vvere opened, and the Doors before the Looking-Glaffes dravvn afide) in all quarters of the Room

Room there vvas nothing but *Suns*,
vvhich by artificial *Refractions* beat upon
the vvhole golden Globe hanging in the
midſt ; and for as much as the ſame
(beſides that brightneſs) vvas poliſhed,
it gave ſuch a Luſtre, that none of us
could open our Eyes, but vvere therefore forced to look out at Windovvs till
the Globe vvas vvell heated , and
brought to the deſired effect. Here I
may vvell avovv that in theſe Mirrours
I have ſeen the moſt vvonderful Spectacle that ever Nature brought to light ;
for there were Suns in all places, and the
Globe in the middle ſhined yet brighter,
ſo that, but for one twinkling of an
Eye, vve could no more indure it than
the Sun it ſelf. At length the Virgin
commanded to ſhut up the Looking-
Glaſſes again, and to make faſt the
Windovvs, and ſo let the Globe cool
again a little ; and this vvas done about
ſeven of the Clock. Wherefore vve
thought good, ſince vve might novv
have leiſure a little to refreſh our ſelves
vvith a Breakfaſt : This Treatment
again vvas right Philoſophical, and vve
had no need to be affraid of Intempe-
rance, yet vve had no vvant. And the

Mirac.ſpæi

Prandium
Philoſoph.

K 5   hope

hope of the future joy (vvith vvhich the Virgin continually comforted us) made us fo jocond that vve regarded not any pains, or inconvenience. And this I can truly fay too concerning my Companions of high quality, that their minds never ran after their *Kitchin or Table*, but their pleafure vvas only to attend upon this adventurous Phifick, and hence to contemplate the Creator's Wifdom and Omnipotency. After vve had taken our Refection, we again fetled our felves to work, for the Globe was fufficiently cooled; which with toil and labour we vvere to lift off the Cnain and fet upon the Floor. Now the difpute was how to get the Globe in funder, for we were commanded to divide the fame in the midft. The con-clufion was that a fharp pointed Dia-

Refolutio Globs.

mond would beft do it. Now when we had thus opened the Globe, there was nothing of *rednefs* more to be feen, but a lovely great fnovv-vvhite Egg: It moft mightily rejoyced us, that this was fo vvell brought to pafs. For the Virgin vvas in perpetuall care, leaft the Shell might ftill be too tender. We ftood round about this Egg as jocond as

if

if vve our felves had laid it. But the
Virgin made it prefently be carried _Ovum can-_
forth, and departed her felf too from _didum._
us again, and (as all vvays) locked the
Door to.   But vvhat fhe did abroad
vvith the Egg, or vvhether it vvere
fome vvay privately handled, I knovv
not, neither do I believe it.   Yet vve
vvere again to paufe together for one
quarter of an hour, till the third hole
vvere opened, and vve by means of our
inftruments vvere come upon the fourth
Stone or Floor.   In this Room vve _4. Conclave_
found a great Copper Kettle filled
vvith _yellow Sand,_ vvhich vvas vvarmed
vvith a gentle Fire, aftervvards the
Egg vvas raked up in it, that it might
therein come to perfect maturity. This
Kettle vvas exactly fquare, upou one
fide ftood thefe tvvo verfes, Writ in
great Leters.

O. BLI. TO. BIT. MI. LI.
KANT. I. VOLT. BIT. TO. GOLT.

On the fecond fide vvere thefe three
Words.

SANITAS

SANITAS. NIX. HASTA.

The third had no more but this one Word.

F. I. A. T.

But on the hindermoſt part ſtood an intire Inſcription running thus.

QVOD.

Ignis : Aer : Aqua : Terra :
SANCTIS REGUM ET REGI-
NARUM NOSTR :
Cineribus.

Eripere non potuerunt.
Fidelis Chymicorum Turba
IN HANC URNAM
Contulit.
• Aö.

Now whether the Sand or Egg were hereby meant, I leave to the learned to diſpute, yet do I my part, and omit nothing undeclared. Our Egg being

novv

now ready was taken out ; But it needed no cracking, for the *Bird* that was in
it soon freed himself, and shewed himself very jocond, yet he looked very
Bloody and unshapen : We first set him *Pullus im-*
upon the warm Sand, so the Virgin *plumis.*
commanded, that before we gave him
any thing to eat, we should be sure to
make him fast, otherwise he would give *Vincitur:*
us all work enough. This being done
too, food was brought him, which sure-
ly was nothing else than the *Blood* of the *Pascitur.*
Beheaded, deluted again with prepared *sanguine.*
decollator-
water, by which the Bird grew so fast *um.*
under our eyes, that we well saw why
the Virgin gave us such warning of him.
He bit and scratcht so devillishly about
him, that could he have had his will upon any of us, he would soon have dispatched him. Now he was wholly *black*,
and wild, wherefore other meat was
brought him, perhaps the blood of a- *Sanguine.*
nother of the *Royal Persons*, whereupon *alius Regis*
all his black Feathers moulted again, *pascitur.*
and instead of them there grew out
Snow-*white-Feathers*. He was somewhat
tamer too, and suffered himself to be
more tractable, nevertheless we did
not yet trust him. At the third feed-
ing

Iridefcit.

ing his Feathers began to be fo curioufly *coloured,* that in all my Life I never faw the like colours for Beauty. He was alfo exceeding tame, and behaved himfelf fo friendly with us, that (the Virgin confenting) we releafed him from

Liberatur. vinculis.

gin confenting) we releafed him from his Captivity. *'Tis now reafon (*began our Virgin*) fince by your diligence, and our old man's confent, the Bird has attained both his Life, and the higheft Perfection, that he be alfo joyfully Confecrated by us.* Herewith fhe commanded to bring in Dinner, and that we fhould again refrefh our felves, fince the moft troublefome part of our Work was now over, and it was fit we fhould begin to enjoy our paffed Labours. We began to make our felves merry together. Hovvbeit we had ftill all our Mourning Cloaths on, which feemed fomewhat reproachful to our Mirth. Novv the Virgin was perpetually inquifitive, perhaps to find to which of us her future purpofe

Primus üfus eius.

might prove ferviceable. But her difcourfe was for the moft part about *melting*; and it pleafed her well vvhen any one feemed expert in fuch compendious

Melodia

Manuals, as do peculiarly commend an Artift. This Dinner lafted not above

three

three quarters of an hour, which vve
yet for the moſt part ſpent with our
Bird, vvhom vve were fain conſtantly
to feed with his meat : But he ſtill continued much at the ſame growth. After Dinner vve vvere not long ſuffered
to digeſt our Meat ; but after that the
Virgin together with the Bird was departed from us. The fifth Room was *s. conclave.*
ſet open to us, whither we got too after the former manner, and tendred our
Service. In this Room a Bath was pre- *lvis bal-*
pared for our Bird, which was ſo co- *neum.*
loured with a fine white Powder, that
it had the appearance of meer Milk.
Now it was at firſt cool when the Bird
was ſet into it : He was mighty well
pleaſed with it, drinking of it, and
pleaſantly ſporting in it. But after it
began to heat by reaſon of the Lamps
that were placed under it, vve had e-
nough to do to keep him in the Bath.
vve therefore clapt a cover on the Kettle, and ſuffered him to thruſt his head
out through a hole, till he had in this
ſort loſt all his Feathers in this Bath,
and vvas as ſmooth as a nevv-born
Child, yet the heat did him no further
haim, at vvhich I much marvelled ; for

in

in this Bath the Feathers were quite confumed, and the Bath vvas thereby tin-
ged into *blew*; at length vve gave the
Bird air, vvho of himfelf fprung out
of the Kettle, and was fo glitteringly
fmooth, that it vvas a pleafure to behold it. But becaufe he vvas ftill fomewhat wild, vve were fain to put a col-
Vincitur. lar, with a Chain, about his Neck, and fo
led him up and down the Room. Mean
time a ftrong Fire vvas made under the
Balceum Kettle and the Bath fodden away till
coguitur in it al came to a *blew* Stone, which vve
lapidem. took out, and having firft pounded it,
vve vvere afterwards fain to grind it
on a Stone, and finally vvith this colour to paint the Bird's whole Skin over:
Nevv he lookt much more ftrangely, for
he vvas all *blew*, except the head, vvhich
remained *white*. Herewith our work on
this Story too vvas performed; And we
(after the Virgin with her *blew Bird*
was departed from us) were called up
through the hole to the fixth Story;
6. Conclave. which vvas done too, there we were
mightily troubled, for in the midft a
little Altar, every way like that in the
King's Hall above defcribed, vvas placed.
Upon which ftood the fix fore-mention

ed *particulars*, and he him self (the Bird)
made the *seventh*.   First of all the little
Fountain vvas set before him,   out of
vvhich he drunk a good draught,   aftervvards he pecked upon the *white Serpent*
until she bled mightily.   This Blood
vve vvere to receive into a Golden Cup,
and pour it dovvn the *Birds* Throat,
vvho vvas mighty averse from it,   then
vve dipt the *Serpents* head in the *Foun-*
tain, upon vvhich she again revived, and
crept into her *Deaths-head*, so that I savv
her no more for a long time after.   Mean
time the Sphere turned constantly on,
until it made the desired conjunction.
Immediately the watch Struck one, upon
which there was a going another *conjun-*
ction. Then the Watch struck two.   Finally, whilst we were observing the third
conjunction, and the same vvas indica-
ted by the Watch, the poor Bird of
himself submissively laid dovvn his Neck
upon the Book, and vvillingly suffered
his Head (by one of us thereto chosen
by lot) to be *smitten off*.   Hovvbeit he   *Auis decolla-*
yielded not one drop of *Blood*, till he   *tur.*
vvas opened on the Breast, and then the
Blood spun out so fresh and clear as if it
had been a Fountain of Rubies.   His
                                    Death

Death vvent to the heart of us, and yet
vve might vvell judge, that a naked Bird
vvould ſtand us in little ſtead, So we
let it reſt, and removed the little Altar

Avis combu- away and aſſiſted the Virgin to burn the
ritur. Body (together with the little Tablet
hanging by) to Aſhes, with Fire kindled at the little *Taper* ; afterwards to
cleanſe the ſame ſeveral times, and to
lay them in a Box of Cypreſs-Wood.

Joc. Here I cannot conceal what a trick I
and three more were ſerved ; After we
had thus diligently taken up the Aſhes,
The Virgin began to ſpeak thus. *My*
Lords, we are here in the ſixth Room, and
have only one more before us, in which our
trouble will be at an end, and then we ſhall
return home again to our Caſtle, to awaken
our moſt gratious Lords and Ladies. Now
albeit I could heartily wiſh, that all of you,
as you are here together, had behaved your
ſelves in ſuch ſort, that I might have given
you Commendations to our moſt renowned
King and Queen, and you have obtained a
ſuitable Reward ; yet becauſe, contrary to
my deſire, I have found amongſt you theſe
four (herewith ſhe pointed at me and
three more) *lazy and ſluggiſh Labourators,*
and yet according to my good-will to all and

every one, *am not willing to deliver them up to condign punishment* ; However, that *such Negligence may not remain wholly unpunished, I am purposed thus concerning them, that they shall only be excluded from the* future seventh *and most* Glorious action of *all the rest, and so too they shall incur no further blame from their* Royal Majesties. In what a case we now were at this Speech, I leave others to consider : For the Virgin so well knew how to keep her countenance, that the Water soon ran over our Baskets, and we esteemed our selves the most unhappy of all men. After this the Virgin by one of her Maids (whereof there were many always at hand) caused the Musitians to be fetcht, who where with Cornets to blow us out of Doors with such scorn and derision, that they themselves could hardly found for *laughing*. But it did *particularly* mightily afflict us that the *Virgin* so vehemently laughed at our *weeping*, *anger* & *impatience*, and that there might well perhaps be some amongst our Companions who were glad of this our misfortune. But it proved otherwise. For as soon as we Commodum ejeco. were come out at the Door, the Musitians bid us be of good cheere and follow

L   low

. conclave.

low them up the winding Staires; They led us up to the seventh Floor under the Roof, where we found the *old Man*, whom we had not hitherto seen, standing upon a *little round* Furnace. He received us friendly, and heartily congratulated us, that we were hereto chosen by the Virgin; but after he understood the affright we had conceived, his belly was ready to burst with Laughing, that we had taken such good Fortune so hainously. Hence said he, My Dear Sons learn, *That Man never knoweth how well God intendeth him.* During this discourse the Virgin also with her little *Box* came running in, who (after she had sufficiently laughed at us) emptied her *Ashes* out into another Vessel,

Virgo Lucifera-
Indicatricis-
TJS.

and filled hers again with other matter, saying, she must now go cast a Mist before the other Artists Eyes, that we in the mean time should obey the old Lord in whatsoever he commanded us, and not remit our former diligence. Here-

7.Conclave.

with she departed from us into the seventh Room whither she called our Companions. Now what she first did with them there, I cannot tell, for they were not only most earnestly forbidden

to

to ſpeak of it, but we too by reaſon of our buſineſs, durſt not peep on them through the Cieling. But this was our work, we were to *moiſten the* Aſhes with our fore-prepared *Water till* they became altogether like a very thin Dough. After which we ſet the matter over the Fire, till it was well *beated*, then we caſt it thus hot as it was into two *little* forms or moulds, and ſo let it cool a little (here we had leiſure to look a while upon our Companions through certain creviſes made in the Floor) they were now very buſie at a Furnace, & each was himſelf fain to blow up the Fire with a pipe, and they ſtood thus blowing about it, as if they were ready to looſe their breath. Howbeit, they imagined they were herein wondrouſly preferred before us. And this blowing laſted ſo long till our old Man rouzed us to our work again; So that I cannot ſay what was done afterwards. We having opened our little forms, there appeared two beautiful bright and almoſt *Tranſparent little* Images, the like to which Mans Eye never ſaw, a Male and a Female, each of them only *four* inches long; and that which moſt mightily

Verus labor ſub tecto.

ibor ſpurius in 7. conclavi.

Homunculi duo.

surprifed me, was, that they were not
hard, but limber and flefhy, as other
human Bodies, yet had they no Life:
So that I do moft affuredly believe that
the Lady *Venus's* Image was alfo made
after fome fuch way. Thefe Angeli-
cally fair Babes we firft laid upon
two little Sattin Cufhionets, and beheld
them a good while; till we were almoft
fotted upon fo exquifite an object.
The old Lord warned us to forbear, and
continually to inftill the *Bood* of the
Bird (which had been received into a
little Golden Cup) drop after drop into
the Mouths of the little Images, from
whence they apparently to the Eye
encreafed; and whereas they were before very fmall, they were now (according to proportion) much more
beautiful; fo that worthily all Limners
ought to have been here, and have been
afhamed of their Art in refpect of thefe
productions of Nature. Now they
began to grow fo *big*, that we lifted
from the little Cufhionets, and were fain
to lay them upon a long Table, which
was covered with white Velvet. The
old man alfo commanded us to cover
them over up to the Breaft, with a piece
of

of fine *white double* Taffata, which becaufe cf their unfpeakable beauty,almoft
went againft us ; but that I may be
brief, before we had in this manner
quite fpent the *Blood,* they were already in their perfect *full* growth, they
had Gold-yellow curled Hair, and the
above-mentioned figure of *Venus* was
nothing to them. But there was not
yet any natural warmth, or fenfibility
in them, they were dead Figures, ye-
of a lively and natural colour : and
fince care was to be taken that they grev
not too great, the old Man would not
permit any thing more to be given them,
but quite covered their Faces too with
the Silk, and caufed the Table to be
ftuck round about with Torches. Here
I muft warn the Reader that he imagine not thefe Lights to have been of
neceffity, for the old Man's intent hereby,
was only that we fhould not obferve
when the *Soul* entred into them, as indeed we fhould not have taken notice
of it, in cafe I had not twice before
feen the *Flames* ; However, I permitted
the other three to remain in their be-
lief, neither did the old Man know
that I had feen any thing more. Hereupon

Pulcheri-
mus.

upon he bid us fit down on a Bench
over againſt the Table: preſently the
Veſtiuntur. Virgin came in too with the Muſick and
all furniture, and carried two curious
white Garments, the like to which I
had never ſeen in the Caſtle, neither
can I deſcribe them, for I thought no
other but that they were meer *Chriſtal*,
but they were gentle, and not tranſparent, ſo that I cannot ſpeak of them:
Theſe ſhe laid down upon a Table, and
after ſhe had diſpoſed her Virgins
upon a Bench round about, ſhe and
the old Man began many *Leger-demain*
tricks about the Table, which was done
Spectatores only to *Blind* us. This (as I told you)
luduntur. was managed under the *roof*, which
Deſcriptio was wonderfully formed, for on the in-
tecti. ſide it was arched into ſeven Hemiſphe-
res, of which the middlemoſt was ſomewhat the higheſt, and had at top a little round hole, which was nevertheleſs
ſhut, and was obſerved by none elſe.
After many Ceremonies, ſtept in *ſix* Virgins, each of which bare a large Trumpet, which were rouled about with a
green glittering and burning material
like a wreath, one of which the old
Man took, and after he had removed
ſome

some of the lights at top, and uncovered their Faces, he placed one of the Trumpets upon the *Mouth* of one of the Bodies in such manner, that the upper and wider part of it was directed just against the forementioned hole. Here my Companions always looked upon the Images ; but I had other thoughts; *Usus tubarum.* for as soon as the foliage or wreath about the shank of the Trumpet was kindled, I saw the hole *at top* open, and a brigh_ *stream* of Fire shooting down *the* Tube, *(ite 'x allo veniens);* and passing into the Body : whereupon the hole was again covered, and the Trumpet removed. With this device my Companions were deluded, so that they imagined that life came into the Image by means of the *Fire* of the foliage, for as soon as he received the *Soul* *Homunculi animarra-* he twinckled with his Eyes, howbeit *lio tranl-* he scarce stirred. The second time he *feruntur.* placed another Tube upon its Mouth, and kindled it again, and the Soul was let *down* through the Tube. This was repeated upon each of them *three times*, after which all the Lights were exstinguished and carried away. The Velvet Carpets of the Table were cast together over them, and immediately a tra-

villing Bed was unlocked and made ready, into which thus wrapped up they
were born, and so after the Carpets
were taken off them, they were neatly
laid by each other, where with the Curtains drawn before them, they slept a
good while. (Now was it also time for
the Virgin to see how our other Artists
behaved themselves, they were well pleased, because (as the Virgin afterwards
informed me) they were to *work in Gold*,
which is indeed a piece also of this art,
but not the most *Principal*, most necessary, and best: They had indeed too a
part of these *Ashes*, so that they ima-
agined no other, but that the whole
Bird was provided for the sake of *Gold*,
and that life must thereby be restored
to the deceased) during which we sate
very still, attending when our married
couple would awake, thus about half an
hour was spent. For then the wanton
Cupid presented himself again, and, after he had saluted us all, flew to them
behind the Curtain, tormenting them so
long till they awaked. This happened to
them with very great amazement, for
they imagined no other but that they
had hitherto slept from the very hour

i2

in which they were beheaded. *Cupid,*
after he had awaked them, and renew-
ed their acquaintance one with another,
stepped a side a little, and permitted
them both somewhat better to *recruit*
themselves, mean time playing his tricks
with us ; and at length he would needs
have the *Musick* fetcht to be somewhat
the merrier. Not long after the Virgin
her self. comes : And after she had most
humbly saluted the young King and
Queen (who found themselves somewhat faint) and kissed their hands, she
brought them the two forementioned
curious *Garments,* which they put on,
and so stepped forth. Now there were
already prepared two very curious
Chaires, wherein they placed themselves : and so were by us with most
profound Reverence congratulated ;
for which the King in his own Person
most gratiously returned his thanks, and
again *re-assured* us of all Grace. It was
already about five of Clock , wherefore they could make no longer stay,
but as soon as ever the chiefest of their
furniture could be laden, we were to
attend the young Royal Persons down
the winding Stairs, through all Doors

Conjuges
induunt
vestimenta
ut se conspi-
ciendos præ-
beant.

Conjuges re-
huntur tra-
mare.

and

and watches unto the Ship, in which they inbarqued themſelves, together with certain Virgins, and Cupid, and ſailed ſo mighty ſwift that we ſoon loſt ſight of them, yet they were met (as I was informed) by certain ſtately Ships; Thus in four Hours time they-had made many *Leagues* out at Sea. After five of Clock the Muſitians were charged to carry all things back again to the Ships, and to make themſelves ready for the Voyage. But becauſe this was ſomewhat long a doing, the old *Lord* commanded forth a party of his concealed Soldiers, who had hitherto been planted in the Wall, ſo that we had taken no notice of any of them, whereby I obſerved that this Tower was well provided againſt oppoſition. Now theſe Soldiers made quick work with our ſtuff, ſo that no more remained further to be done, but to go to Supper. Now the Table being compleatly furniſhed, the Virgin brings us again to our Companions vvhere vve vvere to carry our ſelves as if vve had truly been in a Lamentable condition, and forbear laughing. But they vvere alvvays ſmiling one upon another, how-

Muſica

Cuſtos ſenex

Turris cuſtodita a militibus.

Cœna. Hoſpites de 7. et 8. conclavi comeſſantur.

hovvbeit fome of them too fimpathized
vvith us.   At this Supper the old *Lord*
vvas vvith us too, vvho vvas a moft
fharp Infpector over us : For none could
propound any thing fo difcreetly, but
that he knevv hovv either to confute it,
or amend it, or at leaft to give fome
good document upon it.   I learned moft
by this *Lord*, and it vvere very good
that each one would apply himfelf to
him, and take notice of his procedure,
for then things would not fo often, and
fo untowardly Mifcarry.   After we
had taken our nocturnal refection, the
old Lord led us into his Clofets of Rarities, which were here and there dif-
perfed amongft the Bulworks, where
we faw fuch wonderful productions of
Nature, and other things too which
mans wit in imitation of Nature had
invented, that we needed a Year more
fufficiently to furveigh them : Thus we
fpent a good part of the Night by Can-
dle-light.   At laft, becaufe we were
more inclined to Sleep than fee many
Rarities, we were lodged in Rooms in
the Wall, where we had not only coftly
good Beds, but alfo befides extraordinary handfom Chambers , which made
us

Coftos eft in-
fpector.

Laus hujus
fenis.

The old
Mans Clofets

us the more wonder why we were the
day before forced to undergo so many
hardfhips. In this Chamber I had good
reft ; and being for the moft part without care, and weary with continual Labour, the gentle rufhing of the Sea helped me to a found and fweet Sleep, for
I continued in one Dream from eleven
of Clock till eight in the morning.

The Seventh Day.

AFter eight of clock I awaked, and
quickly made my felf ready, being defirous to return again into the
Tower, but the dark paffages in the
Wall were fo many, and various, that I
wandred a good while before I could
find the way out. The fame happened

Hofpites
deponunt
veftes lugu-
bres.

to the reft too, till at laft we all met a-
gain in the neather moft Vault, and habits intirely *yellow* were given us, together with our golden Fleeces. At that
time the Virgin declared to us that we
were Knights of the Golden Stone, of

Salutantur
Equites.

which we were before ignorant. After we had now thus made our felves
ready, and taken our Breakfaft, the
old

old Man prefented each of us with a medal of Gold ; on the one fide ftood thefe Words,

Donantus à lene.

Ars natura miniftra

AR. NAT. MI.

Temporis natura filia.

On the other thefe,
TEM: NA: F.

Exhorting us moreover we fhould entreprize nothing beyond and againft this token of remembrance. Herewith we went forth to the Sea, where our Ships lay fo richly equipped, that it was not well poffible but that fuchbrave things muft firft have been brought thither. The Ships were *twelve in number*, fix of ours, and fix of the old Lord's, who caufed his Ships to be freighted with well appointed Soldiers. But he betook himfelf, to us, into our Ship, where we all were together; In the firft the Mufitians Seated themfelves, of which the old Lord had alfo a great number, they failed before us to fhorten the time. Our Flags were the *twelve Celeftial* Signs, and we fate in *Libra* ; befids other things, our Ship had alfo a noble and curious Clock, which fhewed us

Navis r.

Vexilla 12, fign. Navis autoris libra. Horolog.

us all the *Minutes*.   The Sea too was fo
calm, that it was a fingular pleafure to
Sail.   But that which furpaffed all the

*Facundia
fenis.*reft,was the old Man's difcourfe,who fo
well knew how to pafs away our time
with wonderful Hiftories, that I could
have been content to Sail with him all

*Obvictio
ex arce.*my Life long.   Mean time the Ships
paffed on amain, for before we had failed two hours the Mariner told us that
he already faw the whole Lake almoft
covered with Ships, by which we could
conjecture they were come out to meet
us, which alfo proved true : For as
foon, as we were gotten out of the Sea
into the Lake by the forementioned Ri-
ver, there prefently ftood in to us five
hundred Ships, one of which fparkled

with mere Gold and pretious Stones,
in which fate the King and Queen, together with other Lords, Ladies, and
Virgins of high Birth.   As foon as
they were well in Ken of us the pieces
were difcharged on both fides, and
there was fuch a din of Trumpets,

*Applaufus.*Shalms, and Kettle Drums that all the
Ships upon the Sea capered again.Final-
ly, as foon as we came near they
brought about our Ships together, and
fo

ſo made a ſtand, Immediately the old
Atlas ſtepped forth on the King's behalf, making a ſhort, but handſom
oration, wherein he wellcomed us, Atlas ora-
and demanded whether the Royal Pre- tione exci-
pit hoſpites.
ſents were in readineſs. The reſt of
my Companions were in an huge
amazement, whence this King ſhould
ariſe, for they imagined no other but
that they muſt again *awaken* him. We
ſuffered them to continue in their won-
derment, and carried our ſelves as if it
ſeemed ſtrange to us too. After *Atlas's*
oration out ſteps our old Man, making
ſomewhat a larger reply, wherein he Atlanti
wiſhed the King and Queen all happi- reſpondet
ſenex.
neſs and increaſe, after which he deli-
vered up a curious ſmall Casket, but Regiis con-
what was in it, I know not ; only it jugibus do-
num affert
was commited to Cupid, who hovered Cupido.
between them both to keep. After
the oration was finiſhed, they again let
off a joyful Volle of Shot, and ſo we
ſailed on a good time together, till at
length we arrived at another Shore.
This was near the firſt Gate at which I
firſt entred : At this place again there
attended a great Multitude of theKing's
Family together with ſome hundreds of
Horſes

Horſes. Now as ſoon as we were come
to ſhore, and diſembarqued, the King
and Queen preſented their Hands to
all of us one with another with ſingu-
lar kindneſs ; and ſo we were to get up
on Horſeback. Here I deſire to have
the Reader friendly intreated not to
interpret the following Narration to
any vain glory or pride of mine, but to
credit me thus far, that if there had
not been a ſpecial neceſſity in it, I could
very well have utterly concealed this
honour which was ſhewed me. We
were all one after another diſtributed
amongſt the Lords. But our *old* Lord,
and I moſt unworthy, were to ride
even with *the* King, each of us bearing
a ſnow *white* Enſign, with a *Red* Croſs :
I indeed was made uſe of becauſe of my
Age, for we both had long *grey* Beards,
and Hair. I had beſides faſtened my
tokens round about my Hat, of which
the young King ſoon took notice, and
demanded if I were he, who could at the
Gate redeem *theſe tokens* ? I anſwered in
moſt humble manner, Yea. But he
laughed on me, ſaying, *There hence-*
forth needed no Ceremony ; *I was* HIS
Father. Then he asked me, *Wherewith*

I

Marginal notes:
Honoratus.
inter Comites, ut jutta Regem.

Teſſeras ſol vit ſale et aqua.

Pater.

I had redeemed them ? I replied, with *Wa-* Teſſers ſovis ſale & aqua *ter* and Salt : whereupon he wondred who had made me ſo wiſe ; upon which I grew ſomewhat more confident, and recounted unto him how it had happen-ed to me with my *Bread,* the Dove, and the Raven, and he was pleaſed with it, and ſaid expreſly, *That it muſt needs be,* that God *had herein vouch ſafed me a ſin-gular happineſs.* Herewith we came to the firſt gate where the Porter with the blew Cloaths waited, who bare in his Hand a ſupplication. Now as ſoon as he ſpied me even with the King, he delivered me the *ſupplication,* moſt humbly beſeeching me to mention his ingenuity towards me before the King : Now in the firſt place I demanded of the King, what the Primus Cuſtos fol. 25. quis. condition of this *Porter* was ? who friend-ly anſwered me, *That he was a very famous* Ob viſam Venerem *and rare* Aſtrologer, *and always in high re-* factus por- *gard with the Lord his Father. But having* titor. *on a time committed a fault againſt* Venus, *and beheld her in her Bed of reſt; This puniſh-ment was therefore impoſed vpon him, that he ſhould ſo long wait at the firſt Gate, till ſome one ſhould* releaſe *him from thence.* I repli-ed, may he then be releaſed ? *Yes,* ſaid the King, *if any one can be found that hath as*

M   *highly*

Autor ejus
dem delicti
reus prodi.
tur à porti-
tore.

highly tranfgreffed *as himfelf, he muft ftand*
in his ftead, and the other fhall be free. This
w ord wentto my Heart, for my Confci-
ence convinced me that I was the offend-
er, yet I held my peace, & herewith delivered the fupplication. As foon as he had
read it, he was mightily terrified, fo that
the Queen, who (with our Virgins, and
that other Queen befides, of whom I
made mention at the hanging of the
Weights) rid juft behind us obferved it,
& therefore asked him, what this Letter
might fignifie: But he had no mind that
he fhould take notice of it, but putting
up the Paper, began to difcourfe of other
matters, till thus in about three hours
time we came quite to the Caftle, where

Actus in
arce.

we alighted, and waited upon the King
into his forementioned Hall. Immediately the Kng called for the old *Atlas* to
come to him in a little Clofet, and fhewed him the writing, who made no long
tarrying, but rid out again to the Porter to take better Cognizance of the
matter. After which the young King
with his Spoufe, and other Lords, La-

Virg Lucif.

dies and Virgins fate down. Then
began our Virgin highly to commend
the diligence we had ufed, and the
pains

pains and labour we had undergone,
requesting we might be royally reward-
ded, and that she henceforward might
be permitted to enjoy the benefit of her
commission.. Then the old Lord stood
up too, and attested that all that the
Virgin had spoken was true, and that
it was but equity that we should on
both both parts be contented. Hereupon
we were to step out alittle ; and it was
concluded that each man should make
some possible wish, and accordingly obtain it;for it was not to be doubted,but
that those of *understanding* would also
make the *best* wish : So we were to
consider of it till after Supper. Mean *Ludus Re-*
time the King and Queen for recrea-*gis cum Regina.*
tions sake, began to fall to play together. It looked not unlike Chesse, only it had other Laws ; for it was the
Vertues and Vices one against another,
where it might ingeniously be observed
·with what Plots the Vices lay in *wait*
for the Vertues, and how to re-encoun-
ter them again. This was so proper-*Artificiosè*
ly and artificially performed, that it
were to be wished, that we had the
like game too. During the game, in
comes *Atlas* again, and makes his re-

port in private, yet I blushed all over:
For my Conscience gave me no rest;
after which the King presented me the
Supplicatio portitoris traditum Autori. supplication to read, the Contents
whereof were much to this purpose:
First he wished the King prosperity,
and increase; that his seed might be
spread abroad far and wide: Afterwards he remonstrated that the time
was now accomplished, wherein according to the Royal promise he ought to
be *released*. Because *Venus* was already uncovered by one of his Guests, for
his observations could not lie to him.
And that if his Majesty would please to
make a strict and diligent enquiry, he
would find that she had been uncovered, and in case this should not prove
so to be, he would be content to remain before the Gate all days of his
life. Then he sued in the most humble manner, that upon peril of Body
and Life he might be permitted to be
present at this Nights supper, he was
in good hopes to spye out the very Offendor, and obtain his wished freedom.
This was expresly and handsomly
indicted, by which I could well perceive his ingenuity, but it was too
sharp

sharp for me, and I could well have
endured never to have seen it. Now I
was casting in my mind whether he
might perchance be helped through my
wish, so I asked the King, whether he
might not be released some other way ?
No, replyed the King, because there is
a special consideration in the business.
However, for this Night, we may well
gratifie him in his desire; so he sent one
forth to fetch him in. Mean time the
Tables were prepared in a spatious
Room, in which we had never been before, which was so compleat, and in Triclinium
such manner contrived, that it is not preciosus.
possible for me only to begin to describe mum.
it. Into this we were conducted with
singular Pomp, and Ceremony. Cupid Cupido ira-
was not at this time present. For (as nerem vilam
I was informed) the disgrace which had ab aauore.
happened to his Mother, had somewhat
angred him. In brief, my offence, and
the Supplication which was delivered
were an occasion of much sadness, for
the King was in perplexity how to Etiam Rex
make inquisition amongst his Guests, condolet.
and the more because thus even they
too, who were yet ignorant of the
matter, would come to the knowledge

M 3   of

of it. So he caufed the Porter himfelf, who was already come, to make his ftrict furveigh, and shewed himfelf as pleafant as he was able. Howbeit at length they began again to be merry, and to befpeak one another with all forts of recreative and profitable difcourfes. Now how the treatment and other Ceremonies were then performed, it is not neceffary to declare, fince it's neither the Reader's concern, nor ferviceable to my defign. But all exceeded more in art, and human invention, than that we were overcharged with drinking. And this was the laft, and nobleft Meal at which I was prefent. After the Bancket the Tables were fuddainly taken away, and certain curious Chairs placed round about in circle, in which we together with the King, and Queen, both their old Men, the Ladies and Virgins, were to fit. After which a very handfom Page opened the abovementioned glorious little Book, when *Atlas* immediately placing himfelf in the midft, began to befpeak us to the enfuing purpofe. That his Royal Majefty had not yet committed to oblivion the fervice we had done him,

Lætitia difcumbentium.

Poft cœnam obligantur eruifes legibus fuis.

him, and how carefully we had attended our duty, and therefore by way of retribution had elected all and each of us Knights of the Golden Stone. That it was therefore further neceſſary not only once again to oblige our ſelves to-wards his Royal Majeſty, but to vow too upon the following Articles, and then his Royal Majeſty would likewiſe know how to behave himſelf towards his liege People. Upon which he cauſed the Page to read over the Arti-cles : which were theſe.

I. You my Lords the Knights, ſhall, ſwear, that you ſhall at no time aſcribe your order either unto any *Devil*, or Spirit, but only to God your *Creator*, and his hand-maid *Nature*.

II. That you will Abominate all Whoredom, Incontinency and Un-cleaneſs, and not defile your order with ſuch Vices.

III. That you through your Talents will be ready to aſſiſt all that are wor-thy, and have need of them.

IV.

IV. That you defire not to employ this honour to wordly Pride and high Authority.

V. That you fhall not be willing to live longer than God ₁ will have you.

At this laft Article we could not choofe but laugh fufficiently, and it may well have been placed after the reft, only for a conceit.   Now being to vow to them all by the King's Scepter, we were afterwards with the ufual Ceremonies inftalled Knights , and amongft other Priviledges fet over *Ig-norance, Poverty, and Sicknefs* ; to handle them at our pleafure.   And this was afterwards ratified in a little Chappel (whither we were couducted in all Pro-ceffion) and thanks returned to God for it: Where I alfo at that time to the honour of God hung up my Golden Fleece and Hat, and left them there for an eternal memorial.   And . becaufe every one was there to write his Name. I writ thus ;

Privilegia.

Summa

Summa Scientia nihil Scire.
Fr, *CHRISTIANUS ROSENCREUTS.*
Eques aurei Lapidis.
Anno. 1459.

Others writ otherwise, and truly each I am poftu-
as feemed him good. After which we lantur de-
were again brought into the Hall, pofitiones
optionum.
where being fate down, we were admonifhed quickly to bethink our felves
what every one would wifh. But the
King and his party retired into a little,
Clofet, there to give audience to our
wifhes. Now each man was called in
feverally, fo that I cannot fpeak of any
man's proper wifh, I thought nothing
could be more praife-worthy than in
honour of my order to demonftrate
fome laudable vertue. And found too
that none at prefent could be more
famous, and coft me more Trouble than
Gratitude. Wherefore not regarding Autor op-
that I might well have wifhed fome- tat libera-
tionem por-
what more dear and agreeable to my titoris e
felf, I vanquifhed my felf, and conclud- gratitudine.
ed, even with my own peril, to free the
Porter my Benefactor. Wherefore being

ing now called in, I was firſt of all demanded, whether, having read the ſupplication, I had obſerved, or ſuſpected nothing concerning the offendor? upon which I began undauntedly to relate how all the buſineſs had paſſed. How through Ignorance I fell into that miſtake, and ſo offered my ſelf to undergo all that I had thereby demerited.

Audit rege confirens. The King, and the reſt of the Lords wondered mightily at ſo un-hoped for confeſſion, and ſo wiſhed me to ſtep aſide a little. Now as ſoon as I was called for in again, *Atlas* declared to me, that although it were grievous to the King's Majeſty, that I whom he loved above others, was fallen into ſuch a miſchance, yet becauſe it was not poſſible for him to Tranſgreſs his ancient uſages, he knew not how elſe to abſolve me, but that the other muſt be at Liberty, and I placed in his ſtead, yet he would hope that ſome other would ſoon be apprehended, that ſo I might be able to go home again.

Audit ſententiam. However, no releaſe was to be hoped for, till the Marriage Feaſt of his future Son. This Sentence had near coſt me
my

my life, and I firſt hated my ſelf and
my twatling Tongue, in that I could
not hold my peace, yet at laſt I took
courage, and becauſe I conſidered there
was no remedy, I related how this Porter had beſtowed a token on me, and
commended me to the other, by whoſe
aſſiſtance I ſtood upon the Scale, and
ſo was made partaker of all the hon-
our and joy already received. And _Laus benefi-_
therefore now it was but equal that I _cij portito-_
ſhould ſhew my ſelf grateful to my _ris._
Benefactor : and becauſe the ſame could
no way elſe be done, I returned thanks
for the ſentence, and was willing gladly
to ſuſtain ſome inconvenience for his
ſake, who had been helpful to me in
coming to ſo high place. But if by
my wiſh any thing might be effected,
I wiſhed my ſelf at home again, and
that ſo he by me, and I by my wiſh
might be at Liberty. Anſwer was
made me, that the wiſhing ſtretched not
ſo far. However I might well wiſh him
free. Yet it was very pleaſing to his
Royal Majeſty, that I had behaved
my ſelf ſo generouſly herein, but he
was

was affraid I might still be ignorant, into what a miserable condition I had plunged my self through this my curiosity. Hereupon the good man was pronounced free, and I with a sad heart was fain to step aside. After me the rest were called for too, who came jocundly out again, which was still more to my smart ; for I imagined no other, but that I must finish my life under the Gate. I had also many pensive thoughts running up and down in my Head, what I should yet undertake, and wherewith to spend the time, at length I considered that I was now old, and according to the course of nature, had few years more to live : And that this anguish and melancholy Life would easily dispatch me, and then my door-keeping would be at an end : And that by a most happy Sleep I might quickly bring my self into the Grave. I had sundry of these thoughts. Sometimes it vexed me that I had seen such galant things, and must be *robbed* of them. Sometimes it rejoyced me that yet before my end I had been accepted to

all

all joy, and should not be forced so shamefully to depart. Thus this was the last and worst shock that I sustained: During these my Cogitations the rest were ready. Wherefore after they had received a good night from the King and Lords, each one was conducted into his Lodging. But I most wretched Man had no body to shew me the way, and yet must moreover suffer my self to be tormented, and that I might be certain of my future function, I was *Autor accipit Annulum.* fain to put on the Ring, which the other had before worn. Finally, the King exhorted me, that since this was now the last time I was like to see him in this manner : I should however behave my self according to my place, and not against the order : Upon which he took me also in his Arms, and *kissed* me, all which I so understood, as if in the morning I must sit at my Gate. Now after they had all a while spoken friendly to me, and at last presented their Hands, committing me to the divine protection ; I vvas by both the old Men, the Lord of the Tovver, and *Atlas* conducted into a glorious *Autor des-* Lodging

_odging, in vvhich ſtood three Beds, and each of us lay in one of them, where we yet ſpent almoſt tvvo, &c.

Here are wanting about two Leaves in quarto, and he (the Author hereof) whereas he imagined he muſt in the morning be Door-Keeper, returned home.

FINIS.